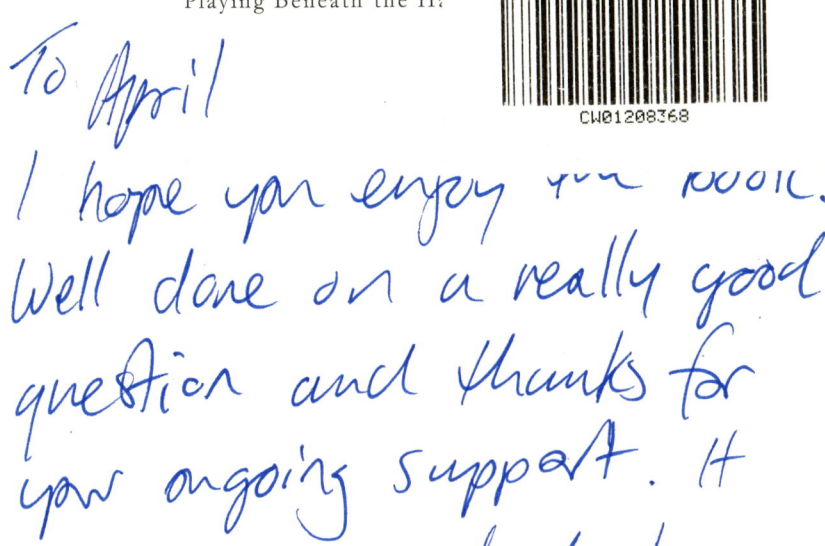

Playing Beneath the Havelock House

Jon Lawrence

This book was first published in 2015
by Create Space for Little Eden Books
First edition 2014.
© 2015 Jon Lawrence / Little Eden Books
Little Eden Books
Keepers Cottage
Low Road
Walpole Cross Keys
King's Lynn
Norfolk
PE34 4HA

The right of Jon Lawrence to be identified as the author of this work has been asserted by him in accordance with the Copyright, Designs and Patents Act 1988

All rights reserved. No part of this publication may be reproduced, stored or introduced into a retrieval system, or transmitted, in any form, or by any means (electronic, mechanical, photocopying recording or otherwise) without prior written permission of the publisher. Any person who does any unauthorised act in relation to this publication may be liable to criminal prosecution and civil claims for damages.
All rights reserved.
ISBN:
ISBN-13:

DEDICATION

This book is dedicated to my wonderful wife Kerry-Ann.

CONTENTS

	Acknowledgments	vii
1	Highway One	1
2	The Ferry	19
3	School	31
4	Watching Possums	39
5	Reading Poems	48
6	Korero (Talk)	57
7	Harry's Place	67
8	Maui & the Goddess of Death	74
9	Swimming in the Sounds	84
10	Fury, Fire and Stars	106
11	Truth & Trusts	116

12	The Search	129
13	Waiting Rooms & Revelations	141
14	Confrontations	154
15	New Beginnings	168
	About the Author	174

Jon Lawrence

ACKNOWLEDGMENTS

I would like to thank the following people for their support, guidance and inspiration; Kerry-Ann and the boys. Sandy & Claire Mears, Stef & Debbie Judd, Sarah Chalke, Nik Storm Gamble, Donna Reid, Chris Skinner, Michelle Deyna-Hayward, Jo Butler, Neil & Tim Finn, Lisa Gerard, Paul Theroux and the people of Havelock, New Zealand.

Jon Lawrence

1. HIGHWAY ONE

Darkness. Eyes closed. An echo of a father's whisper travels through the blackness. It has the rich tones of happiness and the melodic chimes of pure, unadulterated love – a love that can never be silenced. As Dylan Thomas tells us, Death shall have no dominion. The true rule, the only rule, is that of love.

'There is more than this, more than now, more than forever.'

White walls, white floors and white doors. Even the bed sheets were devoid of colour, with the exception of a dull, brown trim on the duvet cover. Dai and Bronwyn had spent the night among the sterile hues of the Hartford Inn since arriving at Auckland Airport the previous day, having wearily weaved through the customs shops selling kiwi key rings, possum-fur handbags and T-shirts sporting New Zealand ferns. All very predictable. After a twenty-five hour flight the only thing that raised a smile for Dai was a sweater which bore the slogan, 'What goes on in the sheep pen, stays in the sheep pen!' For a Welshman on the other side of the world it was a quaint little reminder of what he and Bronwyn had left behind.

Bronwyn made the bed while Dai settled the bill with a beautifully blonde receptionist. She was young, slim and attractive but, with her over-confident manner and provocatively flirting eyes, seemed to know she was beautiful, and as such she was, to Dai at least, profoundly ugly. By the time he returned to room forty-one Bronwyn had restored the place to its former blandness, complete with gleaming white porcelain in the bathroom and crease-free towels. As they made one last scan of the hotel room for any belongings, the only sign that anyone had been there were two miniature plastic milk pots and two damp teabags in the waste bin.

They loaded the suitcases into the car and within minutes they were on Highway One, the road which would lead them the three hundred miles to Wellington and the ferry which would take them to Picton. As they travelled everything seemed still. Bronwyn noticed that there was no wind at all, not even a whispering breeze to rustle the leaves on the trees which were lightly scattered among the long stretches of green farmland that accompanied the journey. The only whispers of any note were echoes of a lullaby softly sung to a child in his hospital bed as chemotherapeutic medicines were pumped into his veins. Hush little baby don't say a word... Indeed, Ieuan never said a word, not of any real note. He was a stoic little boy who never complained, never moaned and was never angered by the hand that fate had dealt him. To the very end he seemed grateful for each and every breath. As Bronnie, as she was nicknamed by Dai, looked out of the car window and watched the white lines of the highway come and go, she would have given anything to be able to sing to Ieuan again.

The stillness extended to the car. The atmosphere was oppressive like the muggy still before a summer storm. The air inside the car was thick with words that could not be spoken and others which had left scars on their recipients. Both occupants had said things to the other that they had regretted and which could never be taken back. So as they passed the exit for Papakura and continued south, the best thing for them both to do was to say nothing at all.

The lack of motion seemed to extend to the landscape and living world around. The sheep in the fields that lined the highway seemed to stand motionless or lay on the ground. Even the lambs, far from frisking and frolicking, seemed content to sit close to the safety of their mothers. Even a huge eagle, which rested on a fence post on the perimeter of the same field and could swoop down and take the young as easily as the leukemia had taken Ieuan, was statuesque. And the beautiful rolling hills had lost all their movement. Bronnie could have been forgiven for thinking they weren't moving at all.

'You okay?' asked Dai.

'Yep,' replied Bronnie without moving an inch.

'Do you want some music on?'

'It's up to you.' She continued to stare out of the window. 'I don't mind.'

'Well, what do you fancy?'

'I don't mind.'

'You choose, we can have the radio on if you like or I have some CDs in my flight bag. There's Springsteen, U2, Beatles, or Crowded House might be a good idea…'

'I don't care!' snapped Bronnie.

Dai gripped the steering wheel a little tighter and tried to retain his cool. He had been used to these kinds of eruptions from Bronnie but knew that it was only really her grief which was coming out. He tried not to take it personally, but sometimes he did wonder if he would ever be able to make her happy again.

'I'll put something easy on.'

He reached behind the driver seat to the flight bag in the footwell, rummaged around for a while before pulling out a selection of CDs which were then placed on his lap while he drove. He picked out a disc marked "Mix" and placed it in the player. Bronnie turned around and picked the remaining discs off his lap and told him to concentrate on the road.

The music began. The tinny, swirling sounds of an electric guitar strumming gently came through the speakers and the liquid tones of Neil Finn came seeping into the heart and memory of both Dai and Bronwyn. There is freedom within, there is freedom without, try to catch the deluge in a paper cup. The song by Crowded House was one of Ieuan's favourites and Bronnie used to sing it to him at night to help him sleep. But the first lines of Don't Dream it's Over had haunted Bronnie ever since Ieuan's death. The image of catching the deluge in a paper cup seemed to sum up so much for Bronnie - the torrents of pain and discomfort which smothered a child so fragile, the overflowing grief, the tidal wave of sadness that spilled out of her heart, the flood of anger which drowned her character and drenched her relationship with Dai. As the chorus kicked in the pain became unbearable once again.

'Why did you put this song on the disc?' she asked angrily.

'I'm sorry, I didn't...'

'You know how I feel about...'

'I know, I said...' The interruptions came thick and fast as if both were trying to get through the discomfort of their conversation as quickly as possible.

'Just turn it off, please!' Bronnie turned away once more and continued to look out of the window. Dai obliged her.

'I'm sorry,' he implored, but Bronnie ignored him.

The December sun was setting by the time they arrived in Taupo. Bronnie had fallen asleep in the car while Dai continued the drive south. The silence in the car had made concentrating difficult so he'd resorted to counting lorries to help relieve the boredom and tiredness. Moving trucks counted as one point, stationary ones were awarded half. Having wearily made his way through the last mile or so along the main road through the town, which weaved around the shore of Lake Taupo, Dai turned on to a back road and finally made his way to the Lakeside Motel. Dai turned the key out of the ignition and the car shuddered to a halt. He rested his head on the wheel and closed his eyes. He could quite easily have slept there and then. After a moment or two Bronwyn stirred. She opened her eyes gingerly and looked around to get her bearings.

'We're here,' said Dai.

'Yes, I can see that.' She began to gather her handbag together. 'Why did you let me sleep so long? I won't sleep tonight now.'

Dai watched her exit the car and wondered if he could say or do anything right.

There is a contention that men need to make love to feel loved and women need to feel love to make love. The irreconcilable contradiction was in evidence that night in another uninspiring bedroom. As Bronnie stepped softly out of the bathroom and into the bedroom, stripped of the make-up which masked her saddened face with light foundation, delicate eyeliner, subtly pink lipstick and blusher to expose her already defined cheekbones, Dai smiled at her and beckoned her into bed.

'I need a hug,' he said.

'Hang on a minute, I just need to take off my nail varnish.'

'Can't you do that in the morning?'

'No, we won't have time,' she snapped.

'Why? What's the hurry?' He sat up in bed and felt his romance ebb away. 'I thought the idea was to take a slow, steady drive to Wellington.'

'I just don't want to hang around.'

Dai waited for Bronnie to finish taking the colour off her fingernails then opened the sheets once more to invite her in.

'Hang on, I need to do my toenails too.'

Dai sighed away his disappointment reclined back down beneath the covers and closed his eyes.

'You know where I am if you need me,' he said wearily.

Eventually, after what seemed like a lifetime, Bronnie slipped beneath the sheets and turned on her side, her back facing Dai's hopeful stare. She reached out to the dusty bedside lamp, fumbled for the switch and plunged the room into darkness.

Dai felt his loneliness so acutely as he listened to his wife clear her throat and sniff lightly. Her body was like the apple hanging from a the tree in the Garden of Eden, so tempting, so beautiful, yet to touch or taste Bronnie's lips would lead to repercussions. However, Dai needed assurance. He needed to know that she still had enough love for her husband to allow him to touch her. He knew there was some love there, somewhere, but where? How strong was it? It was as though their love was a series of binding ropes, which although had held them together through the death of Ieuan, had become knotted and tangled in their grief. The move to New Zealand was an attempt to find time and space to weave their love in and out of the complicated entanglements, to reconnect with each other properly.

Dai moved in to hold Bronnie who was curled up on her side, her hands between her thighs. He slotted his knees in behind the back of her legs, reached his hand over to her slight and slender midriff and pulled her in close. He noticed that her body was free from the scent of perfume, which she always used to wear in bed. Still, he placed his nose into the long red hair and inhaled as if trying to breathe her in to his lungs, into his mind, into his heart. He kissed her on the shoulder, his stubble catching on her soft nightgown, but there was little reciprocation. Finally, he slid his hand slowly but purposefully beneath her clothes and touched the angle of body and breast.

'Don't. I'm tired,' she said with an emptiness which filled Dai's heart

He retracted his hand and felt the humiliation, loneliness and disappointment run through his veins.

'You need your sleep too,' she added, 'it's going to be a long drive tomorrow.'

Dai rolled on to his back, opened his eyes and watched the kaleidoscope of colours and shapes present themselves to him in the pitch-black darkness.

The next morning as the summer sun crept through the window of the motel room and onto Bronnie's face, the alarm burst into a nagging, chiming din. She reached over and fumbled for the switch to end the cacophony and relaxed for a moment. She stretched, yawned, cleaned the sleep from her eyes and turned over to find Dai was gone. Dragging herself up, she sat bolt upright and called for her husband, but there was no reply. She stepped out of bed and made her way into the living area and kitchenette before looking out of the window to the empty car park outside. In her confusion she ambled over to the kettle and flicked the switch on. By the stainless steel sink there was a scrap of paper with Dai's handwriting. It read, "Gone to lake. Everything's ready. Back in a bit." She looked around and the room was spotless. By the kettle Dai had placed a teacup with a teabag inside ready for her daily infusion of caffeine. She headed back into the bedroom, opened the closet and saw the cases packed and ready for their departure. Dai had evidently been up early.

She wandered around the hotel room. With no packing to be done there was little else to do, so she ambled aimlessly through the sterile rooms. She stopped in the main living area and looked at a traditional Maori painting. It was complete with long, colourful, elegant swirls of black and red paint. She didn't understand what it meant; she only knew that she liked it. After putting on her makeup and running the straighteners though her hair to the sound of hissing and sizzling, she sat on the bed. Opening up the bedside drawer she found a copy of The Bible. The cover was immaculate, indicating to Bronnie that nobody had so much as touched it in years. Why should they? What good does it do? What good did it do for her in the past? As she flicked indeterminately through the wafer-thin pages her mind began to wander. She began to hear voices. They were the mumbled rumblings of a doctor talking to a number of young medical apprentices in a long corridor in Sully Hospital. Her eyes glazed over and she saw the dull winter light trying to force its way though tall Dickensian windows in the huge greystone wall hospital, its white hues fusing with the piss-yellow tones from the long fluorescent lights clinging to the ceilings. She saw the doctor dismiss his students and walk toward her. From her side she felt a warm hand take hold of her fingers; it was Dai.

'Mr and Mrs Ifans,' he said with deep and mournful tone. 'Would you like to come to my office?'

'No!' said Dai 'If you have something to say just say it.'

'I really think it would be better if we…'

'Just tell us,' interrupted Dai.

A long pregnant pause. 'Ieuan has leukemia.'

Bronnie felt Dai squeeze her hand tighter.

'I'm very sorry...' the doctor hesitated, '...there is nothing we can do.'

The words echoed inside Bronnie's head, as did her own long, agonizing scream as it carried through the corridor and through her heart and mind. Her eyes refocused on the present and she looked down at the Bible in her hand. She grimaced at it with disdain and dropped it in the wastepaper bin at the side of the bedside dresser.

There was a gentle breeze blowing along the surface of Lake Taupo, hardly enough to register a ripple. Dai sat at the water's edge, his knees pulled up to his chest and a black jumper tied loosely around his neck. In the distance white wisps of summer cloud were vanishing around the snow-capped peak of Mount Ruapehu, the active volcano an hour or so south of Taupo. He sighed, placed his head on his knees and closed his eyes and heard the echoing voice of a little Welsh child.

'Daddy,' he said sweetly, 'Why is the sand black?'

'Because there is a little man who runs up and down the beach early in the morning with a paintbrush who covers the whole beach in black paint!'

Ieuan laughed, heartily, 'No, don't be silly, Daddy!'

'I'm serious! His name is Colin! Colin Butterbottom.'

'Daddy, stop it!' the laughter continued. 'You're being silly!'

'No, it came from a volcano.'

'A volcano?'

'Yes.'

'Which volcano?'

'I don't know, but about twenty-five thousand years ago there was a big explosion and all the earth and sand got burned and so it looks black.'

The voices drifted away into Dai's mind as he picked up a handful of fine blackened sand and allowed it to seep through his fingers. On the water a boat was sailing leisurely, the gentle breeze in no particular hurry to pull it anywhere fast. Dai had always wanted to sail. There were many things he had wanted to do but the last two years had taken all of his dreams from him. Most of his days during that time had been taken up on the children's ward where the only time that mattered was the present. However, despite knowing that Dai and Bronnie had made the most of their last years with Ieuan – trips to the zoo, walks around Cosmeston Lakes feeding the swans and ducks, laughing, singing – he couldn't find solace in that. He had promised that he would one day take Ieuan out sailing but the leukemia had made a liar of him.

'You left me a note,' said Bronnie, startling her husband, 'but I think I knew I'd find you here.'

'Oh, I just needed some air.'

'You get much sleep last night?'

'Yes,' he lied, 'plenty thanks.'

'D'you want me to drive today?'

'No, it's okay.' He stood up and dusted the sand off his trousers and then off the palms of his hands. 'Shall we go?'

Dai put on his mask of happiness and walked purposefully past Bronnie, who could see straight through the disguise.

Highway One once again stretched out before them and the drive was, as ever, silent. When they had previously travelled through New Zealand they were in awe of the landscape, the scale of the mountains, the lusciousness of the colours, the ferns of emerald green, but as Dai steered wearily the world around seemed to lose its wonderment. As the hours past lethargy began to fill the car as if it was creeping in like a poisonous gas through the criss-cross air ducts on the dashboard. By the time they entered Tiahape, the quaint little town where they had stayed on their previous journey, Dai was exhausted. A libation was required but, as there was still some way to go, they both had to settle for a coffee in the Brown Sugar Café.

Once again, the couple retread the steps of their previous journey by visiting the timber-clad building. Stepping inside to a flash-flood of memories, Dai took a seat by the window while Bronnie placed the order at the counter before joining him. Dai rubbed his eyes hard with the butt of his hand, pressing and twisting as if trying to wring out all of his lassitude.

'You alright?' she asked.

Dai yawned and stretched. 'Yep, I'll be okay.'

'I'll drive the next bit, so you can get some sleep.'

'I can't sleep in the car.'

'Try!' she insisted.

'I'm okay!'

'Well, let me drive anyway,' she sighed, 'I'm bored shitless. I think I have counted all of the sheep in New Zealand!'

'How many?'

'More than Wales!'

Dai laughed, 'Well I'll be okay then!'

'Pervert!'

Finally, they both shared a moment of lightheartedness just as a young waitress came with their food. She placed the coffees on the table.

'There you go folks!' she said cheerfully.

'Thanks very much,' said Bronnie.

'Oh, you guys are from England,' said the waitress with an amiable and lyrical New Zealander's twang.

'Wales actually,' replied Dai.

'Oh, close enough!' laughed the waitress.

Dai was well aware that to make the comparable statement that Kiwi's all sound like Australians would probably be pounced upon with justified vociferousness. However, he held his tongue. He liked her. He remembered her from the last time they stopped in Tiahape, and clearly she had a moment of recollection too.

'You know,' she said as she popped the milk down, 'you guys seem really familiar.'

'Yes, we've been here before,' said Dai.

'Here?' she asked 'In Tiahape?

'In this very café.'

'Really?' she said incredulously.

'Yes,' said Dai, 'we were here a couple of years ago, just before Christmas.'

'Oh, didn't you come with a little boy?'

Bronnie's heart sank. 'Our son, Ieuan.'

'Oh, yes!' The waitress clicked her fingers in realization. 'He used to wear that lovely blue cap.'

'That's right,' said Dai. 'You've got a good memory.'

'Oh, well he was a real sweetie. I couldn't forget a little face like that. Where is he now?' she asked innocently.

There was a moment of awkwardness. Bronnie bowed her head.

'Uhm… He passed away.'

'Oh!' The waitress's face dropped. 'Oh, I am so, so sorry.'

'No, it's fine,' said Dai.

'Oh, I am such a mumbling…'

'Honestly, it's okay. I'm just happy you remembered him.'

'I certainly did, he was a darling.' The waitress looked at Bronnie with kindness, but also in search of forgiveness. Bronnie didn't move. There was a long awkward pause. 'Well if there's anything else I can get you, just let me know.'

The waitress left awkwardly while the two consumed their beverages. The brief moment of humour was gone and the grief was, once again, all too real. As Bronnie watched the cars rushing past the window, north and south along Highway One, she wondered if the grief would ever end. Would every second of hope be shadowed by a minute of despair? Would every hour spent laughing be eclipsed by a day spent crying? She knew there would never be a time limit on grief but wondered if its severity would, at least, be subject to impermanence.

The rest of the break took place, once again, in silence and soon they were back on the road. This time Bronnie took the wheel while Dai tried to get some rest. As he reclined his passenger chair back and pulled his coat up over his chest and shoulders, Bronnie questioned him.

'How much were the drinks?'

'Nothing.'

'What?'

'Nothing,' he said. 'The waitress wouldn't let me pay.'

'Why not?'

'I don't know, Bronnie. I think she felt guilty.'

'Guilty?'

'Or maybe she just felt sorry. I think it was her way of offering belated condolences.'

Bronnie became agitated. 'And you were happy with that, were you?'

'With what?'

'With the fact that she pitied you?'

Dai rolled the chair back up. 'Oh, for goodness sake, it wasn't like that.'

'You're happy to take charity are you?'

'No, I just...'

'Just what?' demanded Bronnie, shaking her head in disgust. 'We're not a charity case?'

'It wasn't charity, it wasn't pity... it was human kindness.'

'Kindness?'

'Yes, kindness,' said Dai firmly. 'What's your problem?'

'Oh well, let's just go all out and see what we can get out of our dead child. A new car perhaps!'

'I'm not talking to you while you are like this.' He put his chair back once again and closed his eyes. Bronnie was still ready for a fight.

'Like what?' she shouted. 'Like what?'

Dai ignored her and tried to get some sleep but from out of the corner of his half-opened eye he could see her seething, gripping the wheel so tightly that he feared her knuckles would burst through the skin.

On a long and interminable section of straight road near Parparaumu the rain lashed down. The road began to flood and the windscreen wipers struggled to cope with the deluge. Bronnie moved her nose closer to the windscreen as if trying to look through the freshwater cataract cascading down the glass, her squinting in intense focus. She looked to her left to see Dai fast asleep. Feeling tired and jetlagged, the argument about the free coffee was still playing on her mind. Her anger was still simmering but Bronnie entertained the idea that she might also have been in the wrong. She couldn't see the middle ground, the grey areas between right and wrong, happy or sad. For too long the world was black and white. When Ieuan was alive they all lived a life which was blissfully happy. Days were filled with laughter, nights with Dai were filled with love and romance. Then when Ieuan died the days were filled with endless tears, like the torrent of rain falling down the windscreen, and during the nights she would lay in the same bed as her husband but would be a million miles away. Then as the fork-lightening split the skyline Bronnie heard a little voice behind her singing.

'I hear raindrops, I hear raindrops.' It was Ieuan's soft voice. 'Pitter-patter raindrops, pitter-patter raindrops....'

Bronnie's heart sank and she felt the tears emerge from the corner of her eyes. She accompanied the voice in song and the tears ran down her face, over her lips and gathered to a point on her chin.

'Hark, don't you? Hark, don't you? I'm wet through! So are you!' The sound of Ieuan's laughter came through the din of the car engine and the rain. Bronnie looked in her rear-view mirror and saw Ieuan smiling and laughing in his car seat. Instinctively she turned round and screamed.

'Ieuan!' she yelled at the top of her voice, waking Dai who leapt up from his slumber, looked out of the window and saw that Bronnie was heading for the wrong side of the road and into the path of the oncoming traffic. He quickly turned her around and yelled at her. Bronnie took immediate evasive action and steered the car away from the approaching traffic, but in the process lost control of the vehicle. It proceeded to spin around and around violently until it came to a stop in the grass verge at the side of the road. The car shuddered to a halt. As the episode came to an end all that could be heard was the sound of heavy breathing and rain continuing to tip-tap on the roof of the car.

'You okay?' asked Dai, trying to catch his breath. Bronnie did not reply. She held on to the steering wheel tightly, her distant gaze undisturbed by her husband's words. He repeated.

'What?'

'Are you okay?'

Bronnie paused for a moment looking at the back seat once again. This time it was empty. 'I saw him, Dai!'

'Saw who?'

'I heard him too. He was singing, just like he used to. Just like we used to.'

'I don't understand.'

'It was Ieuan,' she said. The flow of tears resumed once again as she reached for her husband's embrace. 'It was Ieuan! It was Ieuan!'

Dai held her with all the love he had as the storm continued outside and the windows in the car began to mist.

'I'm sorry!' she implored penitently. 'I'm so sorry.'

'It's okay, it's okay.' He kissed her on the head, 'We'll be okay. I promise.'

2. THE FERRY

After an unscheduled night in yet another sterile motel room, this time in Wellington, Dai and Bronwyn drove into the dark hull of the huge ferry which would take them across the Cook Strait to Picton. The bow doors shut behind them and they headed up a spiral staircase to the first deck where the café was situated. Bronnie finished off her tea while Dai left her to get some air on one of the upper decks. The observation deck was on the top of the ferry. The wind on top was wild, although the sun was shining through sparsely scattered white clouds in the sky.

Dai watched the last views of Wellington disappear into the mist behind him, before moving to the front of the vessel and looking forward. Ahead lay the port of Picton and a long winding road which would take them west to the small town of Havelock. Dai and Bronnie had, by some strange stroke of luck or fate, successfully purchased the very house that they had stayed in with Ieuan when they last visited New Zealand. Dai had reservations about going to that house. He feared that, far from recalling the happier times they had spent together as a family, painful wounds might reopen – never to heal. However, Bronnie felt that she would be closer to her departed son in that house than she would in South Wales. They had paid well over the asking price for the house to ensure that their bid was accepted. They had sold their house in Penarth, a great grey-stone house which had four huge bedrooms which was left to them by Bronnie's mother after her death. They achieved an excellent price upon its sale and this helped to fund the purchase of the small house in the hills which overlooked the waters of Havelock and Pelorus Sound. They even had enough money to ask the seller to leave most of the furniture in the house. Money was no object, but loneliness was.

Dai then made his way to the safety barrier at the back of the ship and leaned over, looking at the waves below. He looked back and saw the huge 'V' of the ferry's wake spreading a surge of water east and west. He looked the other way, to the front of the boat and watched a pod of dolphins playfully leaping in and out of the water.

'Daddy,' said a little voice in the back of his mind, 'When we swim with the dolphins will they bite me?'

His own response echoes though his head, as though carrying through the halls of a great cathedral. 'No! You silly thing, of course they won't.'

'Why not?'

'Because you, my boy, are not particularly tasty.'

The sound of young laughter ensued. Dai closed his eyes and remembered their day swimming with dolphins around the bays near Picton. He remembered holding Ieuan, encased in a bright yellow life jacket, laughing in his arms, the two of them bobbing up and down in the water while the inquisitive dolphins swam around and beneath them. He remembered the big splashes of seawater stinging his eyes as the graceful animals leapt out of the sea and came crashing into the wavelets once more. His eyes were still stinging when he opened them and awoke from his reverie, but this time the discomfort was due to the wind and the renaissance of a tear. His eyes were open and the grief was back, acute as ever. As the wind blew on the empty observation deck, Dai leaned forward and looked at the waves below. They were inviting, enticing and he marveled at their simple beauty. Each undulation, each wave, ever-changing and beguiling, hypnotised him and sent him into a deep stare. The stare focused his attention beneath the surface, beyond the darkest depths fathoms down and into a world where all of the pain would be gone. He reached out his hand to the top rung of the safety barrier and placed his foot on the bottom. One leap would be enough to see him down into the waters. The dark but comforting thought was entertained for a moment, but he knew that one more tragedy would be more than Bronnie could bear. He stepped back down from the brink, took a deep breath and went to find his wife... to tell her that he loved her.

Soon the lush, emerald-green mountains, which rose out of the sea like gods and created winding tributaries that would lead to Picton, came into view. In the sheltered bays and picturesque alcoves, seals could be seen basking in the gentle sunshine before sliding effortlessly into the sea. There was a fever of excitement onboard the ferry. Children became increasingly animated as their parents began to gather all their belongings ready for the drive onto dry land. Stewards took their safety positions and the shutters on the gift shop were drawn down. Dai and Bronnie made their way back down into the darkness of the car hold and soon the bow doors opened and sunlight burst through like a supernova.

The road west to Havelock was winding and frightening. Sharp bends and steep drops down the mountainside made for a slow and cautious journey. Dai was weary and his lassitude made his hands cling tighter and tighter to the steering wheel. Soon the narrow exit through emerald green shrubs and foliage came into view and Dai turned right down a dirt track which finally led to their destination.

'Home, at last,' said Dai.

The house at Havelock was a simple yet stunning abode. A board and batten home which protruded out of the hillside. The front reached out into the sky and was supported by a dozen thick cylindrical timber stilts, reducing in length as they crept up the hillside. Beneath the protrusion was a patch of scrub ground, unkempt and something of an eyesore. However, it was this scruffy outside area which held the most precious memories for Dai. After unloading the car and emptying the suitcases Bronnie went for a sleep on the bed, while Dai went and sat down beneath the house, shaded from the December sun. In front of this area was a tiny patch of grass before a dense forest of shrubs and trees which carpeted the mountainside. Dai took his red cap off his head and allowed his wavy blonde hair to seek out the wandering breeze. He sat on the scruffy incline and looked up at the underside of the timber floorboards. Mulish spider webs clung to the corners and swayed gently in the wind. The rest of the garden around the perimeter of the house was smart but unremarkable. This was Ieuan's den, his special play area where he would talk to his imaginary friend, play hide and seek with Bronnie and make movies with Dai. He recalled an argument with Ieuan who wanted to spend the night beneath the house. When Dai declined his request Ieuan had told him that he was the worst daddy in the world. The outburst was out of character for the little boy and was not said with any real conviction, but Dai remembered how hurt he had felt.

Dai spent half an hour beneath the house and allowed his mind to wander. He had hoped it might wander in the direction of a new story for his next novel. His publisher in London was eagerly awaiting a new children's story following the success of his last offering. Alas, nothing was forthcoming beyond the memories of his time with Ieuan. Even the poetry that he wrote for his own solace had dried up. Then, as he was listening to the melodious call of a visiting chaffinch, he heard Bronnie call him in for tea. As he rose and turned to go inside he heard a faint rustling in the bushes beyond the lawn. Believing it to be his imagination he turned around again and started toward the back door only to hear the noise again. He stopped once more and looked into the bushes. Nothing.

After a restless night listening to the possums on the porch outside, Dai arose early to another beautiful day. The sound of a weka calling nearby filled the air and crept through the open window of their modest bedroom. Bronnie, undisturbed in her slumber, looked beautiful and at peace. Dai looked at her for a moment and smiled before heading into the bathroom to brush his teeth and surreptitiously take his tablet – fluoxetine. Dai had been taking anti-depressants for months but did not want Bronnie to know. She, he decided, had enough to worry about without his mental illness making matters worse. He didn't know if the tablets had any real impact, they could not assuage the pain of his grief, but he dare not think about his life without them.

The bungalow, which had an open plan kitchen and living area, benefited from windows on three sides, offering almost uninterrupted views of the natural beauty outside – the rolling hillsides of luscious green, the deep blue skies and the water rolling through the sounds. A skylight allowed the sun to come through the roof. Dai made his way into the kitchen and began to fill the kettle. As he did so he looked out of the window and once again saw a movement in the bushes below. As he looked a little deeper, he could see the bushes parting as something, or someone, made a path hastily through the undergrowth. Dai was lost. It couldn't have been a possum as they are primarily nocturnal. His concentration was broken as the kettle overflowed. He turned off the tap then made his way onto the porch, which overlooked the garden and the beauty beyond. Nothing.

Later that morning, as Bronnie continued to sleep, Dai drove into town to pick up some groceries. The Four Square Supermarket was quiet for a Saturday morning, nothing like the heaving hoards of people which seemed to cram into the aisled metropolis of the giant supermarkets in the UK. Dai much preferred this more quaint and personal affair. The supermarket, although small was crammed to the rafters with comestibles and household essentials like Aladdin's Cave… and just as dark. There were no windows in the shop and the only natural light that made its way into the store came from the single door at the front. Dai wandered up and down the aisles with the speed that only men seem to achieve when shopping. In his haste, as he turned the corner of an aisle, he walked firmly into a man coming in the other direction, knocking the goods out of his hands. Dai apologised profusely and began to help the man pick up his shopping, clumsily spilling more groceries along the way. As they both stood up together Dai saw the intimidating face of a large Maori man. His face was highly decorated with traditional blue swirls and spirals which covered most of his features in perfect symmetry. However, behind the artwork Dai could see his anger and, for a moment, feared reprisals. Dai flinched as the man teetered on the edge of his indignation, but just as the man seemed certain to erupt, he pulled back from the brink and without speaking a word took his remaining groceries from Dai.

'I really am sorry,' said Dai 'I'm afraid I just didn't see…'

Before he could finish his apology the man was on his way. As he walked down the aisle Dai noticed the man's huge muscles bulging out of his weightlifting vest, the gargantuan calf muscles, gigantic feet which were barely contained in flip-flop shoes and was mightily relieved that nothing serious came of his clumsiness.

Dai returned home to see boxes scattered ad hoc around the living room. Their belongings had arrived from the UK and Bronnie had started the process of unpacking. There were relatively few boxes, partly due to the expense of transporting them from one side of the world to the other, but mainly because Dai and Bronnie had decided to leave as much of their old life behind as they possibly could. The unpacking was conducted in complete silence which became increasingly uncomfortable as the morning went on. Bronnie put some music on. The haunting tones of Neil Finn and Crowded House came through the stereo singing Four Seasons in One Day. Boxes were emptied and the contents placed in their new homes; Bronnie's art, pictures she had painted – including one of Ieuan - were placed under the bed, while Dai's books were erected in a number of winding towers inside the walk-in wardrobe in the spare bedroom. Photograph albums were placed in bedside drawers and clothes were hung and folded neatly. Finally they came upon a shoebox with Ieuan's name on. Dai started to peel off the sticky tape from the edges of the box.

'What do you want me to do with this?' he asked.

'Don't open it,' said Bronnie.

'Why not?'

'Just… don't.' She took the box off him and placed it high on a shelf in the cupboard. 'Not yet.'

Later that afternoon Bronnie gathered her teaching materials together and set about preparing for her first day teaching at Havelock School. There were only about sixty pupils at the little school so Bronnie would be teaching a number of age groups. She opened her tan-brown leather satchel, a hand-me-down from her mother, and placed her essentials inside – pens, pencils, calculator, ruler, compass, protractor, stopwatch, notepads and a picture of Dai, Ieuan and herself.

Dai left Bronnie alone with her work, picked up his poetry notebook and laptop then headed outside to sit beneath the house. He lifted the screen on the computer and opened a file marked, 'new book'. It was empty, as was his imagination. He tried to recall some of the stories he had made up when he was last beneath the Havelock house with his son. The secret den, as Ieuan called it, was home to many interesting characters and worlds. Dai had told him that, at night, talking possums and kiwis would make their way beneath the house and get up to all kinds of adventures. It kept Ieuan amused then, but it all seemed so weak now.

As the morning progressed Dai looked out over the garden and allowed his mind to wander. As a lecturer, he had told his writing students that writer's block was an essential part of being an author. 'One cannot always be on output,' he used to say, 'at times one must be on input.' Ideas need to come in before they can go out. So he did what he told his students to do – look at the world. He had a rather Proustian view on life, one which inclined him to look at the world rather than simply see it, in the same way a composer might listen to music rather than merely hearing it. Life, and all of its magic, was in the detail. As such, he watched a blackbird, one of the many avian species introduced by European settlers, scouring the lawn in search of food. Following behind was a dull brown chick, just out of the nest waiting for its food. He watched the father stop in his tracks and lower his head into the grass. Within a few seconds he began to tug at an earthworm beneath the surface. He tugged and heaved at the wriggling invertebrate which stretched like a line of rubber before succumbing to the assault. The father carried the worm in its deep yellow beak and placed it in its infant's gape. The simplicity and the beauty of the moment took Dai's breath away and, almost without knowing it, he began to write.

It doesn't need explaining
It doesn't have to make sense.
It shouldn't take a bearded scientist
To offer a defence.

No need for academia
Or dryly written texts,
No need to know the Latin names
Of all the birds and insects.

There's no need to hold views
About how all this was created -
Evolution or creation?
Endlessly debated.

You could write an article in a journal
With lots of clever words,
That are only really of interest
To other learned nerds.

All that wasted time,
With your head stuck in a book
And all you really had to do
Was to sit in the garden and… look.

Dai sat back and read through the poem, which he titled Uncomplicated, and basked in a moment of self-satisfaction. Just then he detected another movement in the foliage at the end of the garden. Once more Dai looked at the situation but could see nothing.

'Hello,' he said in as authoritative a voice as he could muster. 'Who's there?'

Another rustle occurred, this time to his left. Dai changed the direction of his approach and headed left. He inched closer to the edge of the bushes and his heart began to pound relentlessly. He had never been one for sudden frights and as another movement was detected he began to feel decidedly uncomfortable. He reached out his shaking hand and parted the leaves. The wind died down, the birds seemed to stop singing and even the rattling sound of the crickets appeared to cease. All he could hear was his heartbeat and the sound of the blood rushing through his ears. Another rustle. Another step. Another quivering, shivering breath. Then right at his feet a possum sprinted out from the greenery at lightening speed.

'Jesus Christ!' Dai shouted.

He watched the possum disappear up the garden as he fought to retain his breath. The possum turned around at the top of the garden and stared at Dai, who was convinced he was being mocked by the animal.

'I'd better not catch you laughing at me,' he said 'or I'll make a bloody handbag out of you.'

3. SCHOOL

Dai kissed Bronnie on the cheek and handed her the packed dinner for her big day. He wished her luck and assured her that she would be fine. She offered a faint smile and left him standing alone in the kitchen. It was a short drive to the school, no more than five minutes, over the Kaituna River and the surrounding marshes and into Havelock. Bronnie was one of the first to arrive at the school. She parked the car and walked to the main entrance of the white wooden-clad school. It was a single, open plan building which housed the sixty or so pupils with space to spare. She stood outside the building, her briefcase in her hand, and looked at the school for a moment. It was very different to the large infant, junior and secondary complex which she had left in Cardiff. There you could hide away easily and there were some staff whose names she never got to know. Here it would be very different. There were only three teaching staff, of which she was one, a headmistress and a caretaker.

'Ah, you must be our new arrival,' said a tinny but friendly gentleman's voice. 'Mrs Ifans, I presume?'

'Yes, I am the new reception teacher.'

The man shook her hand and through the lines on his aging, weathered face offered a kindly smile.

'I'm George, I am the caretaker here. If there is anything you need, you come to me and I'll sort things out for you.'

'That's very kind,' said Bronnie.

'Anything at all.'

'So,' said Bronnie making polite conversation, 'you are the man I need if all my shelves fall down?'

George took off his navy blue cap, placed it in the back pocket of his grey, paint-stained overalls and ran his fingers through his thinning silver hair.

'Yep, and if I can't do it Ruru will have a go.'

'Ruru?'

'He's my assistant.'

'You have an assistant?'

'Yes… oh, and speak of the devil.'

Ruru came out from the reception area. He was the very same giant of a man that Dai had walked into in the supermarket. Bronnie, like Dai, was intimidated by his stature and by the bold tattoos on his face and body. George introduced Ruru who merely nodded. His greeting was as distant as it could be; there was no handshake, no smiles, not even a, "hello". He was a silent but formidable character. George on the other hand, seemed to have no fear.

'Right,' he said bossily, 'go and finish painting the railings.'

Ruru was silent, but headed off slowly to complete his chore, staring at Bronnie as he left.

'Well, come on then, get a move on,' said George. He turned to Bronnie. 'Don't you worry about him now missy, he's all show.'

'He seems very angry.'

'Well that's because he doesn't really want to be here.'

'Then why is he here?' asked Bronnie.

'It's part of his conditions.'

'Conditions?'

'Yeah, his parole conditions?' said George.

'Oh, I see.'

'You see he has been allowed out on parole, on the condition that he does some community service.'

'What was he in prison for?'

'Dunno.' George popped his hat back on. 'I can't imagine he's any danger to you or the children though, or they wouldn't have put him here in the first place.'

'I suppose so,' said Bronnie nervously.

'He's a moody soul, but he won't do you any harm.'

It was break time when Bronnie finally met the headmistress, Mrs Anders. Having knocked cautiously on the door and made her way into a bland, colourless office, she saw the corpulent Anders writing at her desk. She continued to make notes as Bronnie entered, a needless show of superiority.

'I'll be with you in a minute,' she said with pomposity. Finally she lifted her gaze and greeted Bronnie.

'My dear Mrs Ifans.'

'Mrs Anders,' they shook hands, 'hello.'

'How are you settling in?'

'Fine thanks.'

'Okay, this is probably as good a time as any to go over a few ground rules. I expect you to be presented in a manner befitting a member of my staff. In other words I want you dressed for a business. Education is a business. I don't want to see phones in your hand during school time and please make sure you have all your teaching resources. I expect you to be here by, at the latest, eight O'clock. You'll leave no earlier than five. I wish to be kept informed of everything that happens in the classroom…'

Bronnie wondered when the conditions of her employment would end. Far from the friendly face who had greeted her on a PC conference interview, Anders now seemed to be little more than a dictator who liked the sound of her own voice.

'…and most important, keep your private and work life separate. Do not bring your problems at home into the staffroom or class.'

Bronnie could feel an anger swelling inside. 'Do you have any objections to my wearing glasses for reading,' she said, doing her best to disguise her sarcasm. 'They are suitably plain.'

'My dear girl!' She stood up and wandered over to the window in her austere office. She then sat on the front of the desk and stared down at Bronnie, who unflinchingly stared right back. 'I know it might seem rather strict, but one must set the correct example for the children; they are, after all, our customers.'

Bronnie bit her tongue. 'Yes, Mrs Anders.'

The two stared at each other, two adversaries sizing each other up, looking for a weakness, searching for the chink in the other's armour. Anders casually picked a piece of invisible fluff off the lapel of her scrupulously clean pin-striped jacket and smiled insincerely.

'Well, my dear, if there is anything you need, please let me know.'

Bronnie stood up and walked out of the office in silence.

After meeting the other two teaching staff at the school, Miss Havers – a young petite girl, just out of university – and the greying Mrs Simpson, Bronnie went out into the playground during her lunch break to watch the children playing in the sun. As her eyes surveyed the playground she caught a glimpse of Mrs Anders watching her like a hawk from behind the blinds of her office window. Bronnie looked away and muttered insults at the woman under her breath. She watched the pupils running freely and laughing in the sunlight. It had been a while since she had last been in a school following her compassionate leave and subsequent resignation, so it was nice to hear the sweet sound of children playing again. A group of older girls were playing hopscotch, chanting to the rhythms of their hops and skips. Boys were playing tag, chasing each other frantically around the yard, weaving in and out of the dinner-ladies, the hop-scotchers, the children stood talking and the loners, who waited for the ground to eat them up. One such child wandered face-down and aimlessly around the yard before finding a place of solitude by the railings that looked out onto the road outside. Bronnie watched him through the busy crowd and, as he lifted his head, she was captured. She was amazed, delighted and terrified at the same time. The child was almost the complete and perfect double of Ieuan. He had the same straight, light brown hair, the same pale complexion and was about the same height. For a moment her heart stopped. She struggled to catch her breath as she watched him hold on to the railings, like a caged animal that had lost all will to dream of a world beyond his steel bars. Slowly she wandered through the crowd of mayhem to the little boy.

'Hiya!' she said.

The boy jumped. He was frightened. 'I'm sorry,' he said nervously.

'It's okay,' she put her hands out to assure him, 'I just wanted to say hello.'

'Hello.' The boy shuffled nervously.

'What's your name?'

'Harry Stone, Miss.'

'Oh, well it's nice to meet you Harry Stone.' The boy lowered his head once more. 'My name is Mrs Ifans.'

The boy made no acknowledgement. He held on to the railings tightly and looked at the world outside the school.

'What are you doing?'

'Nothing.'

'Well why don't you join in the game, it looks like fun.' He shook his head. 'Who are your friends? Who do you like to play with?'

He shrugged his shoulder while his eyes took a sudden interest in the floor, 'I don't know.'

As he lowered his head, Bronnie noticed the yellow tint of a fading bruise, just below his collar-line. She paused for a moment. The potential seriousness of the injury distracted her from her lightheartedness.

'How did you get your bruises?'

'I didn't even know I had them, I probably got them during rugby.'

Bronnie wondered how on earth he might fail to realise he had the marks on his back. She pulled a little at his collar and revealed yet more bruises.

'They look painful,' said Bronnie. 'Do you want me to take a look at them?'

The boy pulled away, 'No.'

'Just to check everything's okay?'

'I'm fine.' Harry pulled away from her and wandered away, back into his loneliness, while Mrs Anders watched on from her office window, or was it her ivory tower?

Bronnie was glad to see the end of her first day at Havelock School. She needed time to take everything in. Her class was like any other; there were pupils who could and some who couldn't, some who had and some who had nothing, some cute, some irritating. But, overall, she was happy with her collection of quirkies, quiets and quibblers. They had enjoyed story time, which offered Bronnie the opportunity to read one of Dai's entertaining short tales.

However, other thoughts were battling for space in her mind. Mrs Anders' comments about the school being a business had disturbed her. This cold approach to educating had been one of the reasons why she had wanted to get out of teaching in Wales. As a teacher in Cardiff she had been under pressure to get all students to a certain level of academia, to meet targets. She knew of other teachers who marked test papers far too generously and, on some occasions, gave the pupils the answers in order to improve their own statistics. Bronnie hated the emphasis on statistics as it gave the children an erroneous view of their learning which did little for them, except to set them up for a fall.

Ruru, his imposing features and silence, had also played on her mind. She was scared of him. Was it his facial tattoos? Was it his muscular physique or his mysteriousness which made her feel uneasy? She didn't know why she felt scared; she just knew she was scared.

However, clinging hardest to her mind was the encounter with Harry. His physical similarity to Ieuan was uncanny and unnerving. She wondered if the marks were the result of a school bully or worse still, violence at home. The teacher in her wanted to get to the bottom of his injuries, while her maternal instincts, still so acute even after Ieuan's death, were simply telling her to hold the boy, to not let him go and to let him know that he was loved. As she packed her briefcase and headed out to her car she continued to think about Harry and why her emotions were so strong with regard to him. The overriding feeling was one of loneliness, but who was lonelier? Was it Harry or herself?

4. WATCHING POSSUMS

The sun had long since set, yet the red and orange hues from its wake were beautifully evident in the late evening sky. Dai sat outside on the balcony which overlooked the picturesque Pelorus Sounds and listened to the last refrains of birdsong while sipping on a glass of local white wine. Bronnie was in bed fast asleep, exhausted after her first week of teaching in months.

As the darkness rose in the clear night sky, Dai heard the rustling in the bushes below and watched as a family of possums made their way onto the lawn. He ambled quietly down below the house and slowly sat down on the grass. To his surprise and joy, the possums remained. For an hour Dai sat as the lights faded and watched the animals wander around the garden. He knew that, to many, these furry friends were little more than a domestic nuisance, responsible for rummaging through bins, eating rare birds like the Kea and some have linked them to the spread of bovine tuberculosis. However, all he could feel was happiness as he watched two joeys play-fighting in the grass while their mother watched on, her large eyes occasionally reflecting the light from the rising moon. With each tumble and fall of the mischievous joeys, he found himself laughing harder and harder. He was surprised that the animals were so tame, so unafraid of his presence. Soon the little ones began to tire and one of them climbed aboard the mother and lay face down on her back. If only Ieuan were here to see this. He pulled up a rickety deckchair, sat back, relaxed and continued to watch the playful marsupials as the stars began to shine in the night sky.

The next morning, the crumbly sound of the car pulling away from a dirt track woke Dai. Bronnie was leaving for work. He opened his eyes gingerly and saw, above him, the long lines of wooden beams which made up the underside of the Havelock house. He had fallen asleep in the deckchair and as he raised his head he felt a painful crick in his neck. He spent a moment or two massaging the muscles either side of his spine and as he did so heard a rustle at the end of the garden in the foliage. Assuming his furry friends were once again playing in the cover of the greenery, he got up and went to investigate.

'Well, little ones,' he said, 'you should be asleep by now.'

As he stumbled in a half-daze toward the edge of the lawn, where the emerald bushes began, something or someone leapt out of the bushes with a deafening, wild scream.

'RAHHHH!' yelled the voice.

Dai jumped and fell back in terror, 'Jesus Christ!'

He stumbled back on to the lawn and for a second closed his eyes as his body filled with fear. Just as the nightmare threatened to take hold of his wits, he heard the sound of uncontrollable laughter, that of a child. He opened his eyes and saw in front of him a young Maori boy who would have been no more than seven years of age. He was a slight little fellow with red shorts and a white vest which was clearly far too big for him. On his feet he wore some blue, slip-on sandals.

'Ha ha! I frightened you,' he said from behind a mischievous smile, 'didn't I?'

Dai fought to catch his breath and calm his timpanic heartbeat. 'Really? What gave that away?'

'You screamed!'

'Of course I screamed, you scared the shit out of me.'

'Om!' he gasped, 'you said a swear.'

Dai gulped. 'Not really!'

'Yes you did.'

'No, I didn't. I have Tourette's Syndrome.'

'What's that?'

'It's a condition that many people suffer when little turd comes out from a bush on a quiet morning and proceeds to scream at them. Christ, I near enough soiled myself.' The boy looked confused for a moment, but soon returned to his laughter. 'Where did you come from?'

'From the bushes.'

'Dai rolled his eyes, 'I know that! Where do you live?'

'Down the hillside,' he said chuckling.

Dai looked sternly at the boy. 'It's not funny you know. You could've given me a heart attack.'

'I'm sorry, I was only playing.'

This time the boy looked a little sheepish. Dai calmed down a little and regulated his breathing.

'Who are you?' he asked. 'What's your name?'

'Hemi.'

'Well, Hemi, shouldn't you be getting ready for school?'

'You're worse than my Dad.'

'I don't care, you should be in school, not scaring the sh...' Hemi looked at him, his eyebrows raised, ready to pounce on another profanity, 'sh… sugar out of people like me.'

'I'm going in a bit, school doesn't start for another half hour.'

'So what are you doing here?'

'You new here?'

'Yes.' Dai retired to his deck chair.

'You foreign?' asked Hemi inquisitively.

'Yes I am from Wales.'

'I know Wales, we beat you at Rugby.'

'Yes, well don't get ahead of yourself, we've been beaten by Tonga too!'

'A Pākehā.' Hemi folded his arms confidently.

'A what?'

'Pākehā.'

'And what does that mean?'

'That's what my Dad calls the white people.'

Dai looked perplexed and not a little suspicious. 'Why do I feel like it is an insult?'

'It's not,' he began to mime a drop-goal kick. 'Well, not really.'

'What d'you mean?'

'Well, some people don't like it.'

'Well, are you a friend?'

'Yeah!' He smiled, 'I come in peace!'

'Well, then I have nothing to be offended about, have I? And as for coming in peace, there was nothing peaceful about the way you stormed out of those bushes, you little...'

'Language!' interrupted Hemi.

'...Devil!'

'Anyway, I just came to say hello.'

'Yes, but you didn't say "hello" you said, "RAAAHHH" at the top of your voice.'

Hemi laughed, a sweet innocent giggle which was endearing. He mimed a rugby pass, from left to right.

'You play rugby?' asked Dai.

'Used to. Not anymore. My Dad was a rugby player. Professional! You?' asked the boy.

'I was never really built for rugby. I was always too thin.'

'You're not now though are you?' he said looking at the slight belly protruding over the belt line of Dai's waist.

'You cheeky little sod,' Dai smiled. 'Are you calling me fat?'

'No... I just... I mean...'

'Keep digging mate, Keep digging!' The two laughed. 'No, I used to be really skinny – a bit like you, you scrawny little devil.' Another chuckle. 'My Dad used to say that I was like the gable end of a one pound note! My brother used to say I had muscles like knots in a worm's willy.'

The two laughed heartily, as if nothing mattered.

'What's your name, Pākehā?

'Dai.'

'Oh, that's a strange name.

'It comes from Dafydd which means David. Like David in the bible.'

'Oh,' a moment of innocent confusion and a long pause 'I think I'll call you Pākehā.'

Hemi wandered off back into the bushes, down the hillside and out of view.

'Great!' Dai said to himself. 'I think I'll call you turd!'

The sun had retreated by lunchtime and a cool southerly breeze weaved its way through the Sounds. The coldness had forced Dai inside. He dragged the kitchen table to the French doors so that he could survey, at his leisure, the beautiful views outside. However, Dai knew that such a change in ergonomics could go one of two ways; the peace and serenity might place him in a relaxing frame of mind, which would make him receptive to ideas and thoughts; on the other hand the hypnotic, rolling landscape might make him susceptible to daydreaming, or worse still memories. In truth, memories could apprehend his concentration at any moment – and they all revolved around Ieuan. Any of his senses could be stirred and trigger a recollection of his son. The beeping sound on the microwave brought back painful reminiscences of breathing apparatus and heart monitoring machines being switched off in stuffy hospital rooms. The feel of knitted woolen fabrics, such as the colourful blankets that Bronnie had so studiously made, reminded him of the feel of tiny cardigans, intricately woven together by Dai's late mother. The smell of rain after a thunderstorm evoked images of

Ieuan and him standing at the cliff top in Penarth, overlooking the Bristol Channel and watching the lightning strikes. The taste of salt and vinegar on tightly wrapped portions of chips made him recall family days out at the seaside near Barry Island. The sight of planes made him think of his son. Ieuan had been so inspired and excited by his trip on a 747 that he had told him that he wanted to be a pilot when he was older. A dream stolen.

Dai turned on his computer and saw what every writer despises more than anything – a blank page. The only thing which looked worse was the letter from his literary agent back in London stating that the publishers wanted a copy of his brand new children's book within six months. He wandered the house all day looking for excuses not to write. He made coffee and took his antidepressants, prepared dinner for Bronnie's arrival after school and even did some remedial DIY around the house. Why? Because he simply had nothing to say. Nothing which would have been of any real interest to a child reader. Dai had written a number of children's stories, complete with magical worlds, dragons, maidens, princes, trolls, mythical kingdoms and colourful imaginary landscapes. He had been able to create these wonderful worlds because he had never really left his own childhood behind... or so Bronnie would say. He had been absorbed into the C.S Lewis's Narnia as a child and later as an adult had been swept away by the Christian symbolism which eventually led him to the church.

With thoughts of Narnia firmly in his mind Dai sought out his childhood copy of The Lion The Witch and the Wardrobe. He ran his fingers over the cover gently as though caressing a lover. The book, complete with faded pages and a dedication to his grandfather from the author himself, was handled like a holy relic. It had held memories of his own childhood when the book was passed down to him from his own late father, but now the memories were of Ieuan. He scoured the first few pages and soon began to hear an echo of his own voice reading to his son. As he read, he saw Ieuan wrapped in his arms, in his blue-painted bedroom, listening intently to his own mercurial voice. The section of Aslan's sacrifice in the book, which so clearly alluded to the crucifixion, was being addressed when Ieuan interrupted.

'Daddy?'

'Yes?'

'What will happen to Aslan now that he is dead?'

Dai closed the book, kissed Ieuan on the head and did his best to avoid the question, however the little boy was still insistent.

'We'll find out as we read on, won't we?' said Dai.

He wrapped Ieuan tightly in his bedclothes, carefully tucking the duvet in between the mattress and the bed frame. He kissed him once again and made his way to the bedroom door, but just as he turned out the light, the inquisitive little boy asked one more question.

'What will happen when I die, Daddy?'

Where does one start? Dai and Bronnie had resolved to keep the seriousness of Ieuan's illness from him. They didn't want to frighten him, they didn't want him to give up fighting the illness, but most of all they couldn't say the words. The inability to use words such as "dying" or "terminal" would be tantamount to an admission of the truth. As an author, Dai had made words and language his life, but when he needed them most, they failed him. And he felt bitter about it; perhaps it was this perennial bitterness which would prevent him from writing a single word.

'I don't know, kiddo.' He swallowed hard and took a deep breath, 'I don't know. But that won't happen for a long time yet.'

'Oh, okay?'

'Get some sleep.'

'Goodnight, Daddy.'

'Goodnight, kiddo.'

The sound of the bedroom door shutting echoed long in his mind as Dai came out of his reverie. The lie, as kind as it was, as well-meaning as it had been, was still a lie. His head knew, even now, that it was the right thing to do, yet his heart was still riddled with guilt and penitence. How could he write now? How could he write of rainbows, unicorns, moonbeams and summer days, when, just like Lucy stepping through the wardrobe into the snow of Narnia, all he felt was the coldest winter.

5. READING POEMS

The sound of the early children arriving at the school could be heard from Bronnie's classroom. She went around the room taking all of the chairs down off the tables from the day before, and then filled the children's drinking bottles from the tap. The class was set for the first session so Bronnie spent a moment gazing out of the window. She noticed how some children sprinted through the gates, charged and delighted at the thought of another day with their friends, while others were more pensive. As a child Bronnie would have fitted into the former category. She loved school and was a natural student, while Dai hated school and he became so introverted that he retreated from the crowds into his own world of fiction and literary wonder. Then, as the last children were making their way into the school, she saw Harry lagging behind his Mother who was screaming at him to hurry up. She stared uneasily as she watched Harry stumble and fall, to the consternation of his Mother who was, by now, losing her temper. She ran back to him as he lay on the ground observing the graze on his knee, picked him up roughly by the collar and dragged him to his feet. He was so slight, so slender and so frail. Bronnie feared he might break beneath the force of her hands. She wanted to run out into the schoolyard, pick him up, cradle the boy in her arms and tell him that everything would be alright. Finally, Harry's mother pulled at his hand so hard that, even from within her classroom, she could hear Harry yawp in pain. Bronnie could stand and watch no longer, she stormed out of her classroom armed only with raw emotion and bad language. She pulled open her classroom door – and screamed.

Standing before her was Ruru. His size, his mysterious presence, his silence and the facial tattoos, of which she was still relatively unaccustomed, ignited a fire of fear within her. There was no reaction from Ruru, no apology, no concern or, seemingly, any thought for her whatsoever. Bronnie did her best to make light of the situation but behind the swirls and curls of faded blue lines Ruru was devoid of all emotion. An awkward silence ensued before Bronnie, who by this time had forgotten all about Harry's ordeal outside, finally spoke.

'Uh, was there something that you wanted?'

'Boss says you need a new cupboard door,' he said in a deep yet almost hypnotic, monotonal voice.

Bronnie, still gripped with fear, took a while to respond.

'Boss?' she said. 'I never mentioned it to Mrs Anders.'

'No, my boss,' he said plainly, 'George.'

Bronnie remembered that she had told George about some loose hinges on her cupboard door and then showed Ruru the offending furniture. He looked at the hinge and assessed the situation silently but intensely.

'I'll come back later and fit a new one.'

'Thank you, Mister…' she stopped. 'I'm sorry I don't know your surname.'

A pause. 'People call me Ruru.' He turned and abruptly walked out of the classroom, as the first pupils started to trickle in for morning sessions.

As lunchtime approached Dai sat beneath the Havelock house, his alfresco office (consisting of a notebook, pen and laptop) was unused in the pursuit of his novel. With regard to the required children's book, his mind was empty – devoid of ideas or inspiration. He had lots of things he wanted to write about – he had an entire historic novel, set in the First World War, all planned out in his head - but none of them met the brief of his ever-pursuing publisher and literary agent. Having lectured in creative writing for years to financially support his efforts to find a publisher, he had often told his students that a good writer can write great books when he is in the mood, but a great writer can write a book when he isn't. By that token, he wondered if he was the talented writer his publisher had thought. His first novel had been successful because the muse had been Ieuan. The characters, worlds and stories which had brought him financial rewards had come about simply because he had been able to make a little boy laugh and smile at bedtime. Then, as he was guiltily considering a lunch he knew he did not fully deserve, Hemi once again appeared from the bushes and startled Dai.

'Jesus Christ!' he said. 'Is this going to be your trademark entrance?'

'What?' said Hemi, innocently.

'You shouldn't scare people like that!'

'Oh, sorry,' he said casually. 'What are you up to Pākehā?'

'I'm working!' said Dai abruptly.

'Really? You look like you're sunbathing to me!'

'You cheeky little sod.'

'What?'

'I am not sunbathing, I am actually working very hard indeed and I could probably do without the occasional heart-attack from children springing out from the bushes at the end of my garden!' Hemi shrugged his shoulders while Dai continued his defence. 'Anyway why would I be sunbathing under here?'

'Okay, okay!' Hemi took out a lollipop from his back pocket, peeled off the wrapping and placed it in his mouth, 'D'you want one?'

'No, thank you.'

'Good, 'cause I've only got one!'

'Ha! Ha!' Dai gave a sarcastic smile, 'Quite the comedian aren't you?'

'So, what are you doing here? What do you do?'

'I am an author,' said Dai proudly. 'I write books.'

'What kind of books?'

'Children's books.'

'I hate reading,' said Hemi without any concern about giving offence, 'it's boring.'

'What are you talking about?'

'It's booooring,' he repeated with even more attitude.

'Why?'

'Because!'

'Because?'

'Well I don't wanna sit around for hours staring into a book,' said Hemi. 'It's just a heap of words.'

'Have you ever read a book?'

'I've read a few, at school.'

'And?'

'And it was boooooooring!' Hemi said bursting with nonchalance.

'Did your teachers read to you?'

'Yes, that's why I was bored.'

'Yes, well maybe if someone read you a story with a little feeling,' argued Dai, 'then you might actually enjoy it.'

'Yeah, but they always take so long!'

'Not always!'

'In my school, story-time used to take ages. I'd rather be out playing.' He swung his leg and converted an invisible rugby ball.

'Well, what about poetry?'

'POETRY!' he stuck two fingers down his throat. 'Yuk!'

'Oh, let me guess,' said Dai who was slowly beginning to lose his patience, 'it's boooooooring.'

'Poetry is for girls!'

'Don't be so silly!'

'It is! Fluffy clouds, pretty flowers, all that stuff…'

'I can see you have studied poetry in some depth!'

Hemi, oblivious to Dai's irony, kicked another imaginary ball. 'I hate poetry!'

'Okay how about this?' Dai picked up his tatty notebook and flicked through the pages.

'You're not going to read to me, are you? I may have to kick you!'

'Just listen, you little turd.' Dai began to read.

> *Everyone loves a bogey,*
> *Everyone loves a snot.*
> *Some like them cold in sandwiches,*
> *Some like them nice and hot.*
>
> *Don't try to deny it,*
> *Don't get proper and prim.*
> *Everyone eats their nose grub -*
> *You, me, her and him.*
>
> *Some like them light and crusty,*
> *Like little green crisps.*
> *I like mine garnished with nose-hair,*
> *A sort of slimy Willow the Wisp.*
>
> *My wife prefers them stringy,*
> *Like Spaghetti Bolognaise.*
> *I hide mine in my cabbage,*
> *In my beef roast on Sundays.*
>
> *You see, we all need our bogies,*
> *We all need our greens.*
> *So don't waste them by picking and flicking*
> *Or rubbing the snot in your jeans.*
>
> *You could always pick and roll your snot*
> *Into nice chewy little balls,*
> *Or open your nostrils, tap the top of your head,*

Stick your tongue out and catch what falls.

But you just can't beat a juicy one.
It's like eating a nice green slug.
I wish the hard ones came in packets
And the wet ones came in jugs!

If you are feeling a little adventurous
Then mix in a little ear wax.
It's something of an acquired taste
But a good idea with snacks!

Like a fine wine, snot matures with age
So put a few aside!
Then bring them out on special occasions
With the grub from under your fingernails… fried.

So next time you have a runny nose
Don't get all upset.
The bogey is the bestest food
You're ever likely to get.

By the time Dai had finished performing the last line, complete with funny voices and quirky facial contortions, Hemi was bent doubled, laughing so hard that the tears were rolling down his face.

'That's disgusting!'

'Thank you very much,' said Dai proudly. 'It made you smile though.'

'That was really funny.'

'And not a fluffy cloud in sight,' said Dai

'My teachers never read anything like that.'

'Well of course they haven't. As far as teachers are concerned, school is a repository for adults who have no sense of humour... but don't tell my wife I said that.'

'I have no idea what you said anyway... something about a suppository?'

'No, that's a tablet you put up your bottom.'

'Errrr!' said Hemi covering his mouth in disgust.

'You said it!' laughed Dai.

'Yes but I didn't think you were going to explain it to me!'

Dai was now free from the shackles of his loneliness and creative impediment. This was the first time in a long time he had heard the healing sound of laughter.

'Got any more?' asked Hemi.

'Well, let's see.' He flicked through his notebook once more, 'How about this one? This one is called My Friend Bob L.D. Gooke.

'Don't you mean gobbledygook?'

'No I mean Bob L.D. Gooke!'

'Go on then,' demanded Hemi in anticipation.

I have a friend that no one else can see
And everyday he's here with me.
All I have to do is pretend
With Bob L.D. Gooke my imaginary friend.

Sometimes he's a wizard with a big pointy hat
And a wand to turn me into a bat.
Sometimes he's a really funny clown
With baggy trousers that keep falling down.

Sometimes he's a cowboy from the old Wild West

A ten-gallon hat and a sheriff's star on his chest.
Sometimes he's a diver way beneath the sea.
Diving deep in a spotty submarine.

And when I'm feeling lonely, when I'm feeling sad,
When I'm feeling frightened and everything's bad,
Bob L.D. Gooke is here, right to the end.
You're never alone with an imaginary friend.

Dai closed his notebook and watched as Hemi smiled softly. His face, for a moment seemed reflective and poignant. Dai noticed the change in his demeanour.

'You okay?'

Hemi snapped out of his brief melancholy. 'Do you have an imaginary friend?'

'I think I'm just a little bit old for that.'

6. KORERO (TALK)

The table was set. The candles were lit, the cutlery was carefully placed in course order and the wine, which had been chilling gently in the fridge all day, stood waiting to be opened. In the background the slow movement of Bach's G minor cello sonata, Bronnie's favourite piece, filled the room with romance. The incense sticks infused the air with the potent scent of jasmine. The early evening sun beamed through the windows and cast lengthening shadows across the open-plan living room and kitchen. Rose petals were lined along the route from the door to the dinner table ready for Bronnie's arrival. Determined that the evening should be one of happiness and love rather than bitterness and resentment, Dai reached into his pocket and pulled out a foil tablet package. He pushed the sertraline pill through the silver foil and swallowed it down with a little wine. Then he sat at the table and allowed the anti-depressant's chemicals to find their way to his reeling mind.

By the time Bronnie arrived home, almost two hours later than usual, Dai's dinner had long been consumed and Bronnie's placed unceremoniously in the microwave. As she walked in through the door, throwing her bags and books in a heap on the doormat, she failed to notice Dai sitting at the table. She stumbled, half asleep to the sofa and slumped into its welcoming hold in a heap. Without looking up from the chair she finally spoke.

'I am shattered.'

'Yes, I can see that,' said Dai with one elbow on the dining table, his hand loosely grasping the glass holding the last dregs of wine. 'Busy day?'

'That bloody woman!' she exclaimed. 'She had me in the office going over all of my marks, criticizing left, right and centre! Yes Mrs Anders, no Mrs Anders, three bags full Mrs Anders, kiss my arse Mrs bloody Anders!'

'Just humour her.'

'You're not the one who has to listen to her constant patronizing.'

Dai, by this time, was not in the mood for an argument. 'No, I'm not.'

'What have you been up to?'

'Oh, not a lot,' he replied wearily.

Eventually, Bronnie detected the disquiet in her husband's voice. She looked up from her comfort and finally saw Dai at the table, the candles half the length they had been two hours ago, the wine consumed.

'Oh Dai, did you do all this for me?'

'No, I did it for the bloody possums,' he said sarcastically, yet still with a faint smile on his face.

'I'm so sorry, sweetheart.'

'It's okay,' he said.

'No, it's not, I really am sorry.' She rose from the sofa and made her way to the table. She put her arms around him. 'It was that bloody woman though.'

'Don't worry about it.' Dai broke off the embrace, 'I'll heat your dinner up.'

He set the timer on the microwave and started to reheat the dinner before heading to the bathroom.

'I'm going for a shower,' he said miserably.

As he left Bronnie repeated, 'I'm sorry... I'm sorry.'

That night Bronnie wanted to be tactile, but it was impossible. She wanted to hold Dai, to give him the tenderness he so needed and deserved. She missed his touch, the way he would run his fingers through her hair, the slow strokes of his hand down the bare skin on her back and the way he would write I love you on her chest with his finger. She knew that he wanted to make love to her and hated herself for not obliging him. The grief would not let go of either of them.

The next morning, over a simple breakfast, Dai had resolved to put on a happy face, as his mother would say. He was up early and when Bronnie arrived at the breakfast table her food and drink – a coffee and an orange juice – were presented neatly. Initially the breakfast table was silent and dead. Bronnie had been subdued by her own guilt and Dai was unsure of her response to the previous night's happenings. Nothing was able to ignite the spark of conversation, until Bronnie opened her diary and looked at the week ahead.

'Oh, we're doing story-telling and poetry this week,' she said, finally breaking the silence, 'I was wondering if you might like to come in and talk to the children.'

'What about?'

'About writing,' she replied. 'I thought it might be nice for them to meet a real author.'

'Do you really want them to turn out like me?'

'Oh, stop feeling sorry for yourself.'

Dai arose from the table and cleared away some dirty cups.

'Oh, I don't know!' he said.

'Please, it would really help me.'

'I just don't know what to say.'

'You spend your life with language, with words… and you can't think of anything to say?'

'That's different!' Dai was becoming more and more exasperated.

'Why?' said Bronnie, without missing a beat.

'Because…'

'Because?'

The words and the language failed. 'Oh, alright.'

Dai got up irksomely and as he did so, a foil packet fell to the floor. Bronnie bent down and picked it up and looked at the contents. She knew what sertraline was, having been prescribed it following her own postnatal depression shortly after Ieuan had been born.

'Are these yours?'

'Give them back to me,' Dai snatched them out of Bronnie's hands. 'It's got nothing to do with you.'

'What on earth do you mean?' she said. 'It's got everything to do with me. You are my husband and…'

'Am I?' Dai interjected. Bronnie was taken aback. 'Am I really your husband?'

'I don't follow.'

Dai put the tablets back in his pocket. 'Am I your husband, or am I just the guy who makes the tea? Am I your lover or the man who runs the errands? Am I your punch bag?'

'Why are you saying this? I'm not judging you.'

'Ever since Ieuan died, I have taken on your anger and your grief as well as my own. I have let you hit me, I've let you tell me that I should have been there more…'

'I didn't mean it,' pleaded Bronnie. 'I didn't know what I was…

'… I gave you space, I gave you time and I gave you everything that I thought you needed. And I did it in the hope that someday you might find some place inside you for me - for my grief. I have spent so much time dealing with your grief that I have forgotten all about mine. Now I wake up in the night, numb. I wonder where I put all my sadness and when it will be revisited upon me.'

Dai stormed out of the room, slamming the door behind him. Bronnie stood motionless.

Later that day, Dai had spent a good two hours writing beneath the house, stopping occasionally to feed the crumbs of his sandwich to a visiting chaffinch. He tried to forget the things he had said to Bronnie, but wondered what, if any, repercussions would follow. Unfortunately, he failed to come up with a single line of prose for the children's book his publisher and agent were expecting, but did come up with a pleasing poem. At least he was writing. He was admiring his poetic offering when a little voice came, as ever, through the bushes and on to the lawn.

'What you doing Pākehā?'

'Oh, hello Hemi.' He shut his notebook and closed his laptop. No more writing would take place now. 'I've just been doing some work. Anyway, do you have to call me that?'

'What?' he smiled. 'Pākehā?'

'Yes, that!'

'Why? What's so bad about it? It's just a bit of fun.'

'I do have a name, you know.'

'Okay, fine.' There was a moment of quiet, and Dai could almost see the back of Hemi's head working as he tried to jog his own memory. 'What was your name again?'

'Dai!'

'Oh yeah!'

'For Christ's sake.'

Hemi put his hand to his mouth in disgust. 'Om, you're swearing again!'

'Blaspheming actually!'

'What's that?'

'That's when you take the Lord's name in vain.'

'Do you speak English Pākehā?' He paused, realised the error of his ways and corrected himself.

'When you talk about God or Jesus you have to be respectful?'

'Why?' asked the boy.

'Because…' Hemi raised his eyebrows in anticipation while Dai thought. '…Because you have to.'

'I don't like God.'

Dai was taken aback by the carefree flippancy with which such a profound statement was issued.

'Why not?'

'Because he did so many horrible things.'

Dai retired to his garden chair while Hemi sat at his feet.

'Such as?' asked Dai.

'Well, he sent the flood to kill everyone.' Dai said nothing, rather he allowed the boy to express himself freely. 'He sent the plague to kill all the Pharaoh's children. He even told Abraham to kill his own son.'

'He had reasons for doing those things though.'

'My Dad says that nobody kills for no reason at all. Our ancestors killed animals to eat, they killed people who were going to hurt them. It doesn't mean it's right.'

Dai couldn't argue with such a truth. 'No, I suppose not.'

'I mean, why would he want to take a child?'

The poignancy of the little boy's words suddenly struck Dai like a thunderbolt, almost knocking him off his chair. He felt an icy shudder down his spine and, in the company of the innocent child, felt anger well up within him. Indeed, why would God take Ieuan? Why would he take him away from his family, from the people he loved and who loved him? As the fury threatened to engulf him he slipped into another memory.

The rain was pouring down and the wind whistled through the cemetery. Mourners circled a tiny grave, no more than four feet long, three or four people deep. A melancholic din of teary snivels, gentle weeping and the occasional wail of torment and torture echoed through the air, accompanied by the indeterminate rhythms of raindrops clattering down on umbrellas. He felt the vice-like grip of Bronnie's slender hand as the priest said his piece.

'We come here today to mourn the death, but also to rejoice in the life of Ieuan David Ifans.'

What reasons for rejoice were there? How could one celebrate another day watching a child close his eyes as a needle goes into his arm once again? Why would anyone want to remember the sound of a young boy crying as yet more drugs rushed through his veins?

The priest continued to offer his eulogy as though he had known Ieuan all of his life, claiming that the child was at peace and at one with God.

'Fuck God!' Dai whispered under his breath.

Ieuan was at peace before God sent the cancer to poison him. Dai, in his agonizing reverie, could hear the echoing sound of the priest's standard lines.

'The Lord God, who created the heavens and the earth...'

Indeed, thought Dai, but the very God who created so much beauty and majesty also created Leukemia and parasitic worms that will burrow through the eyeball of an African child. He had always found it hard to reconcile his thoughts about the church, but as he watched his son being lowered into the earth, those thoughts became impossible. The only iota of consolation came in the inevitable thought that God did not exist.

'You okay?'

The sound of Hemi's slight voice disturbed Dai from his recollections and, aware that he had been somewhere else, offered a smile.

'Sorry, I was miles away then.'

'What were you thinking about?' asked Hemi.

'It doesn't matter.'

Hemi, still sat at Dai's feet, picked up a flower from the lawn and twisted it between his thumb and forefinger and watched the centre turn like a kaleidoscope. 'Do you believe in God?' asked the boy.

'That's quite a question.'

'Why?' he shrugged his shoulders. 'Either you do or you don't.'

Dai paused a moment, thinking of a way out of the question.

'Do you?'

'Nope!' Hemi said without hesitation.

'But you said you didn't like God. How can you dislike someone who doesn't exist?'

'Dunno.'

Dai smiled. 'You're quite a box of contradictions aren't you?'

'What are contradictions?'

Dai tried to simplify his language. 'It's a bit like when you say one thing then do another.'

'Oh, a bit like God then.'

'What do you mean?' asked Dai.

'Well, he told everyone not to kill and then killed all those people.'

'Oh, I see. Yes'

'And he told us not to steal.'

Dai was perplexed. 'What did he steal?'

'All those people! He stole them from their families.'

The boy articulated so simply, but exactly, what Dai and Bronnie felt about God; that he was little more than a villain in some great book. As such, the atmosphere lightened and Dai found a moment of consolation, a hint of contentment and, at least, the prospect of happiness.

'Anyway, why aren't you at school?'
'Dentist!'
'You got any more poems or stories?'
'What is this, bloody Jackanory?'
'What?'
'Never mind!' Dai stood up to indicate that their meeting was at an end; Bronnie had left a long list of chores which had to be done. 'Tell you what, next time you come here, you tell me a story.'

'What?' he scowled. 'That's like homework.'

'No, think of it as a gift. I told you a story, now you can tell me a story.'

Dai stood up and made his way back into the house, leaving his little friend, mouth agape and looking somewhat confused on the lawn.

7. HARRY'S PLACE

Bronnie was helping George put some shelving up in her classroom after the children had left late in the afternoon. In George she had found a likeable friend who, like many old people, had a knack for saying how things really were. He would comment on her slight appearance by telling her that she needed to eat more and that she looked like an emaciated stick insect. Such comic honesty made her smile. In a school, and indeed a profession, where one had to be constantly aware of what one was saying and how it was said, it was refreshing to hear such openness.

'So, why did you leave Wales to come here?' he asked directly.

'It's complicated,' replied Bronnie, hoping that would put an end to the conversation.

'I see, running away were you?'

'Not at all!' said Bronnie indignantly.

'Well, there must be some reason for you to pack up everything and move to the other side of the world.'

'I love the way you are completely devoid of subtlety, George.'

'Well, I don't believe in pussyfooting about,' he declared.

Bronnie smiled kindly at him, 'You're a good man George.'

'And you're a lovely girl!' he blushed.

'A girl!' she laughed. 'I' prefer that to a woman. Makes me sound younger.'

'If I was thirty years younger…' he said.

'George, you old flirt.'

'I was telling my wife about you the other night.'

'Oh, you'll have to forgive me George I thought your wife had died, that's what Miss Havers said.'

'Two years now,' he confirmed. 'She had a massive stroke and was dead before I could call an ambulance.'

'George, I am so sorry.'

'But that doesn't stop me talking to her. When you think about it, it makes perfect sense. I mean all those silly sods in church, they still speak to a bloke who died two thousand years ago. So it makes sense that I talk to someone who was with me a couple of years ago.'

'And death shall have no dominion.' Bronnie uttered the words in a staring trance-like state.

'Sorry?' said George.

'Dylan Thomas.'

'I tell her all about my day and I told her you were a pretty little thing. I think she's a bit jealous so you better watch your step!'

Bronnie moved over to George and gave him a kiss on the cheek and embraced him like a father. Then he looked upwards to the heavens.

'Sorry Mable,' he said. 'She overpowered me, darling.'

Bronnie laughed and returned to her chores with George, who changed the subject.

'I understand you've had a few run-ins with Mrs Anders.'

'Who told you that?' asked Bronnie.

'Well, let's just say that in a little town like this you are always within earshot of some gossip or other.' He put a drill mark on the wall in pencil. 'Is it true?'

'I can't stand the woman.'

George laughed, 'No, I heard that too!'

'She's a business woman, not a teacher.'

'Maybe, but just watch her okay, love.'

'What do you mean?'

'Well, put it this way, you don't want to make an enemy of her.' He put a drill mark at the other end of the shelf, which Bronnie held in place. 'She's pretty harmless really, but she can be a bit of a dragon.'

As George proceeded to drill holes into the wall, Ruru entered the room. Bronnie felt an icy chill run down her spine. When George was finished, Ruru spoke.

'What now, George?' he said in his deep dispassionate voice.

'The guttering needs cleaning out above Mrs Simpson's window.'

There was no politeness in George's voice, no friendliness, not even a "please". Ruru said nothing in return, rather he sighed, turned and left the room without complaint. George could see that Bronnie was decidedly uncomfortable.

'He won't hurt you, you know.'

'What?' she said, snapping herself out of her fear.

'He's just a big scary oaf,' he smiled warmly at her. 'He looks big and menacing, but he won't hurt you. Anyway, he's got to be on his best behavior or he'll be back behind bars.'

'I wonder what he did?' said Bronnie curiously.

'Don't know, don't care,' said George insouciantly. 'As long as that gutter gets cleared, that's all that matters to me! Back in a mo, just going to get some screws.'

She looked out of the classroom window and could see, beyond the school gates, Harry sitting alone on a bench. The other children had been picked up long ago by their parents, but Harry, whose feet didn't quite reach the floor, sat swinging his legs back and forth, alone. Bronnie headed out to the street.

'Harry?' The boy was startled. He flinched as though preparing for a heavy blow. 'It's okay! It's only me. What are you doing here?'

'Uh, I'm just...' the boy paused, just as Ieuan used to when he was preparing a little white lie. For a moment it was as though he was sitting right in front of Bronnie.

'Where's your Mother?' The timid child shrugged his shoulders. 'Was she supposed to pick you up? Is she coming to get you, Harry?'

Harry's silence persisted. He gazed nervously at his hands, while Bronnie stared at what looked like fresh bruises on his arms.

'Well, come back into my classroom and I will ring your Mother. Then she can come take you home.'

'No!' he said abruptly.

'Why not?'

'Because... because the car is broken.'

'I see.' Bronnie suspected another lie but made nothing of it. 'Well then, let me take you home, you can't stay out here all night, you need to…'

'No, it's okay,' he interrupted, 'I am going to walk home.'

The boy almost leapt off the bench, gathered his little satchel and began to run away from the school.

'Harry!' she shouted. 'Wait! Come back!'

Harry ran as fast as he could, never looking back once.

That evening Harry, or was it Ieuan, was firmly on Bronnie's mind. As she got in the car to drive home, she began to think about his reaction to her offer to take him home. Something wasn't right and she became increasingly concerned about the boy.

Bronnie knew Harry's address and so resolved to call by and check that everything was okay. As she arrived at the house on Campbell Street, just off Highway Six, she found her way to a little white house. The paint was peeling off the walls, the lawn outside was knee-high and the gate hung precariously off a single hinge. A swing and see-saw were rusting in the long grass and, as she approached the house, Bronnie noticed that the curtains were drawn. There was something eerie about the house and Bronnie felt uncomfortable. A deep breath was required before she was able to knock on the door with any conviction. After a couple more knocks the door was opened six inches and Harry's mother poked her thin white face through the gap.

'Yes?'

'Mrs Stone?'

'Yes, what do you want?' she asked sharply.

'Oh… I… I was just checking that everything was okay?'

'What are you? A bloody social worker?'

'No, I am a teacher?'

'A teacher?'

Bronnie took a step closer and Mrs Stone shut the door an inch or so. 'Yes, I just wanted to check that things are okay?'

'Why wouldn't they be?' she snapped.

'No reason.'

'Then why are you here?'

Bronnie took another deep breath. 'It's just that Harry was alone outside the school this afternoon. I was wondering if you… if you might have forgotten to pick him up.'

Mrs Stone became agitated. 'Just what are you accusing me of?'

Bronnie raised her hands in defence. 'Nothing, it's just that…'

'Why don't you mind your own bloody business? Harry's home, he's safe with me and that's all there is to it. Now good evening!'

Mrs Stone slammed the door shut, leaving Bronnie shaking on the porch.

That night Bronnie and Dai laid side by side in a bedroom consumed with silence and the sad irony was that both had so much they wanted to say. Ever since they had arrived in New Zealand they had avoided talking about Ieuan, at least in any great depth, and hidden their feelings behind work and trivial conversation. As they lay trying to convince the other that they were already asleep, they both thought about the two little boys who had become such a secretive part of their first days in Havelock.

Bronnie could not tell Dai about Harry. She couldn't say that she had seen a little boy so similar to Ieuan for fear that he would think her deluded, and Dai could not speak about Hemi for fear that she would think that he was not grieving for Ieuan. The silence and secrecy was beginning to pull them further apart from each other in a town where they had moved to draw closer and deal with their grief.

8. MAUI AND THE GODDESS OF DEATH

Weeks had gone by. The silences between Bronnie and Dai were prolonged and seemed to stretch into long days of nothing, punctuated occasionally by uncomfortable kisses, strained embraces and yet more nugatory conversation. Bronnie continued to foster concerns about Harry's safety and happiness, while Dai entertained Hemi most nights in the backyard with stories and poems, yet still could not offer a single word to his publisher. Indeed, both children were the escape that Bronnie and Dai needed. Harry gave something Bronnie wanted – the need to be needed, the need to exercise her maternal instincts. Hemi on the other hand, offered Dai the most simple of friendships. The little boy made him smile and he looked forward to his visits every day. Each visit would become a revelation. Dai learned all about the Maori traditions from Hemi and the little boy even took the time to teach Dai the Haka. Hemi's father had been a schoolboy rugby international and had passed on his teachings of the pre-match war call as performed by the All Blacks. More importantly, Hemi had revealed the shoots of happiness to Dai. Though the pain of his own son's death was still in his heart, every now and then Hemi's love, kindness, innocence, his humour and quirkiness, cheekiness, humanity, compassion and sweet simplicity would ameliorate his torment.

One night as the sun was dipping beneath the luscious green mountains that surrounded the Sounds, there was a familiar rustle at the bottom of the garden where Dai sat waiting for another encounter with the possums. Hemi came out of the foliage without his usual spring. He was much calmer, almost melancholic in his stride and he greeted his friend.

'It's a bit late for a visit, isn't it?' said Dai. 'You should be getting to bed.'

'Who are you talking to?' shouted Bronnie from within the house.

'I'm just reading through some of my book,' he replied. 'It's okay, I'll be in in a minute.'

Dai turned back to Hemi, who stood with a composure and equanimity which belied his age.

'I've found a story,' he said softly.

Dai was in jovial mood, happy to see his friend. 'A story?'

'You asked me a while ago to tell you a story?'

'Oh, great.' Dai pulled up the deck chair and invited Hemi to take a seat. 'Well then, you better sit in the storyteller's chair and I'll have the lawn.'

Hemi sat in the chair which seemed to swallow him whole.

'Okay, let's hear it,' said Dai.

'It's an old Maori story which I heard during a tangi. My Dad told it.'

'Tangi?' Dai smiled but was confused. 'What's that?

'A tangihanga,' Hemi replied. 'It's like the Maori funeral.'

The smile lowered on Dai's face as he listened to the little storyteller.

'Have you heard about Maui?'

'No, what's Maui.'

'You mean, "Who?"'

'Okay, who was Maui?'

'He was a Maori god. He was son of Taranga.'

'I see,' affirmed Dai politely.

'One day Maui was talking to his father, Makeatutara and he said that he was unhappy that people have to die. His father told him that all men are doomed to die. All men. Makeatutara said that in the end they just fall like fruit from the tree and the Great Mother of Night, Hinenuitepo picks them up and gathers them in. Maui wasn't happy with that. He said to his father that if Death were to die then all men would live forever.'

Dai sat perfectly still as Hemi continued with his story. He was swept up in his words, which almost seemed rehearsed.

'His father,' Hemi continued, 'said that it was silly to think that way. He said it was dangerous to think that anyone could defeat Death. He told Maui that even he must die, just like a normal person, like you and me.'

Dai shuffled slightly as Hemi moved forward to the edge of his chair.

'But Maui wouldn't listen. He said, "I have beaten fire and calmed the sun. I can beat death too!" But his father said that when he was baptized, he forgot to say all of the words in a special prayer which undid the prophecy.'

'The prophecy?'

'The prophecy that he would live forever?' explained Hemi. 'His father told him again that he would die like everyone else. But Maui still wouldn't listen. His father said that Hinenuitepo would kill him. So Maui said he would have to try and defeat her, but his father said that she was terrifying, beyond his worst nightmares. He said, "She has eyes which you can see flashing out on the horizon between the sky and the land." Maui looked and saw the eyes flashing. Then his father said, "Her teeth are sharp, she has a horrible grin like a barracuda and her hair covers her face like seaweed. She is a monster."'

Dai listened to the boy as the sun disappeared and the coldness of the night fell upon him.

'Anyway,' said Hemi, 'Maui, who was really crafty and sneaky, planned to defeat Hinenuitepo who was asleep in the distance. He was so pleased with his plan to defeat her that he laughed really loud. But it was so loud that his laughter woke Hinenuitepo from her sleep. She thought he was mad to laugh when she was waiting to kill him. Then she went back to sleep.'

'Yes?' said Dai 'What happened next?'

'Well, Maui decided to take some friends from the forest with him, so they could see him go through Death and come out the other side, to show them it could be done. He took robins, tits, warblers and fantails and he said to them, "I will enter Hinenuitepo's body and come out the other end but whatever you do, do not laugh or I will die.'

As Hemi continued his story, the dusk chorus from the robins, tits, blackbirds and warblers crescendoed and seemed to accompany the tale.

'So, eventually Maui found Hinenuitepo asleep in a clearing in the forest. He crept up quietly and signaled silently to the birds not to make a sound. The birds didn't want him to do it, they thought he was mad, but they couldn't say anything. Then Maui took off his clothes until he was naked. Then he made his way into her body – head first! Soon he was half inside. The birds couldn't believe it. It looked so silly, so crazy and some of the birds nearly laughed. After a little while Maui made his was through Hinenuitepo's body until his face could be seen rising up through her open mouth. Well, that was it, the birds burst out laughing just as Maui was about to pass through Death. Hinenuitepo woke up and killed him. She squeezed the life out of him. And, because he failed, we all have to die. We are all walking to Hinenuitepo. All of us.'

Dai was transfixed. The story and the storyteller were something of a revelation and he was silent and motionless as Hemi stood up to leave.

'Anyway, I gotta go, there will be trouble if I'm out too late.'

Hemi walked over the lawn and back through the greenery down the forested hillside before Dai could draw the breath to say goodbye.

The next morning, Bronnie kissed Dai awkwardly on the cheek before heading out to work. As she drove the short distance to Havelock School, her thoughts were solely of Harry. In the weeks since her meeting with the short tempered Mrs Stone, she had noticed Harry becoming increasingly withdrawn and the marks and abrasions on his body more and more common and widespread. He had started to wear long sleeve shirts which covered up the marks, but Bronnie new they were there. The little boy had apparently been excused from PE and swimming for the last few weeks due to a variety of health complaints, but it was clear to Bronnie that this was a ruse to ensure that the marks on his body remained hidden. Bronnie had spent many an hour arguing with Miss Havers, the young teacher in charge of Harry's class. She was reluctant to make waves in her first year as a teacher and refused to pass on the information to Mrs Anders about the boy.

The school assembly that morning was uneventful. Prayers were said and school notices read out to the pupils. As the children left the hall Bronnie watched as Harry trailed at the end of the line of classes heading off to their morning sessions. He was uneasy and held his head low.

'Harry?' she called.

The boy stopped silently in his tracks but kept his head low.

'Harry, can I have a quick word?'

She moved closer to Harry and asked if everything was okay. The child shrugged his shoulders without a single utterance. She lifted his chin gently to look at him and as his pale face rose she noticed another mark this time beneath his fringe.

'Is everything okay, Harry?'

'Yes, Mrs Ifans.'

'How did you get these marks?' The boy said nothing. 'Harry, this is important, how did you get these marks?'

He shuffled uneasily. 'I... I fell off the swing in my garden and banged my head.'

Bronnie new this was a lie. She had remembered the swings in Harry's garden; they hadn't been used for years, as the rust on their frame proved. Bronnie, convinced that something was seriously amiss, let the boy go to his sessions.

At break time Bronnie put her dislike of Mrs Anders to one side and knocked on the door of the Head's office.

'Come in,' said the pompous voice.

Bronnie walked into the office and stood at the desk waiting, as usual, for Mrs Anders to finish her task, and grant her an audience.

'Right, my dear,' she said removing her glasses, 'what can I do for you?'

'It's about Harry Stone.'

She looked confused as she tried to remember who Harry was.

'You'll have to remind me, my dear. I don't remember all of the names of the children in the school.'

This annoyed Bronnie. At her previous school the headteacher made it his task to memorise each and every pupil, even in such a large school. The least Mrs Anders could do, Bronnie thought, was to come out of her ivory tower and get to know the children in her school.

'Harry Stone,' she repeated. 'He is in Miss Havers' class.'

'Continue.'

'I have been keeping and eye on him for the past few weeks or so.'

'Yes?'

'Well, he's been appearing, almost daily, with bruises all over his body.'

'Nobody has said anything to me about this,' said Anders.

'No, exactly! That's why I am here now. Miss Havers is too afraid to make a fuss.'

'It's her responsibility!' snapped the Head.

'Easier said than done. It's her first year as a teacher. She doesn't want to rock the boat.'

'And you think it's abuse? Violence at home?'

Bronnie replied swiftly and positively. 'Yes, I have no doubt.'

'Why?' enquired Anders.

'He has started to hide the marks by wearing long sleeve shirts and...' Bronnie hesitated. She new her next piece of information would very likely put her into hot water.

'Yes?'

'When I went to his house to see if he was okay, his mother answered the door and was less than polite to say the least.'

Mrs Anders rolled her eyes and flung her head back in disbelief.

'You went to the house?'

'Yes, I had to...'

'What the hell were you thinking?' interrupted Mrs Anders.

'I was thinking about the safety of that little boy.' Bronnie became defensive.

'There are proper established channels to go through, Mrs Ifans. You should know that. You can't just call in and accuse a parent of… what did you accuse her of?'

'I didn't accuse her of anything. I just had to make sure things were okay.'

Anders stood up, walked to the window and peeped out over her domain through the gaps in the blinds.

'And you,' she sneered, 'came to the informed and professional opinion that the boy was being abused?'

'No, I came to that opinion as a Mother. I came to that conclusion as someone who works with children every day rather than sitting behind a bloody desk all the time.'

'I beg your pardon!'

'You heard me. How can you possibly see what's going on here? You hardly even see the children.'

'If you're trying to lose your job then you're going the right way...'

'Don't you threaten me,' interrupted Bronnie. 'If you are proved to have let this slide under the carpet, I don't imagine the governors would be too pleased. Who knows? Maybe your job would be on the line as well.'

The two stared at each other, sizing the other one up as though preparing for battle. During the silence which ensued, Bronnie considered how she could possibly tell Dai that she had ben fired after only two months in New Zealand. Finally, Bronnie spoke. Her voice was calmer. An olive branch had effectively been offered, but would Anders take it?

'Look,' she said, 'we both want the same thing.'

'And that is?'

'To know that Harry is safe.'

Anders sat down once again as calm descended upon the office.

'There are rules,' she affirmed. 'We have to follow protocol.'

'Yes but what happens while those rules are being followed? What happens while the procedures are applied? Do you think the abuse…'

'If it is abuse.'

'Do you think it will stop in the meantime?'

9. SWIMMING IN THE SOUNDS

'Have you remembered the workshop today?' asked Bronnie as she poured tea into a large novelty mug at the breakfast table.

'What workshop?' said Dai, looking somewhat perturbed.

'The writing workshop with my class.'

'Is that today?'

'Yes!'

'Oh shit!'

Bronnie sighed. 'You've forgotten haven't you?'

'Can I do it next week?' he pleaded.

'No, I have planned it all out.'

'But what am I going to say to them?'

'Just tell them what you do and how you do it.' Dai began to sulk, while Bronnie tidied the table. 'Smarten yourself up, and hurry up. I need to get going.'

Dai sat alone in the classroom waiting for the children to arrive while Bronnie filled all the water bottles for the tables. His acute sense of edginess was magnified by feelings of clumsiness. He felt like the Big Friendly Giant among the lines of tiny chairs, miniature tables and seemed to be forever ducking his head down so as not to catch a hanging decoration. He wandered around the classroom to calm himself and made his way to the window. He looked out and saw the imposing figure of Ruru emptying the rubbish bins. Despite the distance between them, Dai still felt a coldness run down his spine as he recalled their encounter at the supermarket. Then, almost as if an extra-sensory perception had been triggered by Dai's stare, Ruru halted his cleaning duties and stared straight back into the classroom. He caught Dai's attention firmly and glared back fiercely. A moment of awkwardness ensued before Bronnie spoke.

'You nearly ready?'

'What are they like?' asked Dai, turning nervously away from the window.

'They're like kids,' replied Bronnie, oblivious to his nerves. 'Inquisitive, excitable, sometimes noisy... they're just kids.'

Within a couple of minutes the children had shuffled their way into the classroom and sat down on the square carpet in front of Bronnie's desk. After a quick headcount - all present, Bronnie completed the register quickly with no need to go through all of the names. She placed her hands between her knees and addressed the class.

'Good morning boys and girls.'

'Goooood Mooorrrring Missssuuus IIIfffans!' the class said in rhythmic unison.

'I'd like you to welcome a very special guest of mine. His name is Mr Ifans.'

'Is he your husband Mrs Ifans?' asked Hine, an excitable little Maori girl.

'Yes, he is.' The class tittered and chattered much to the embarrassment of Dai. 'And he has come to talk to you about being a writer. So without further ado, please give him a nice warm welcome.'

The children applauded as Dai, knees shaking conspicuously, took his place on Bronnie's chair while she retreated to the back of the classroom to complete some paperwork.

'Uhh… well… Good morning boys and girls.' Another rhythmic response. 'I am an author. Who knows what an author does?'

A forest of hands shot up, reaching as high as possible with the prospect of arms popping out of sockets a distinct possibility.

'They write stories?' said the red-headed Molly nervously.

'Yes, that's right. Well done. I am also a poet so I earn my money from writing poems as well as books. Now, who likes to read poems.'

The class was as still as the humid air which filled the room. Not a single hand was raised except a little dark hand at the back of the class which belonged to a familiar face; Hemi. Dai noticed him but decided not to draw attention to the boy.

'What's wrong with poetry?' he asked.

'It's boring!' said the brash, curly headed Richie.

'It's boring, is it?' Dai folded his arms. 'So you won't want to hear a silly, funny poem about a killer cat then, will you?'

The class erupted excitedly and begged Dai to read the funny poem, which after a while, he did.

Tommy – The Killer Cat

Another gift from Tommy waits by the kitchen door,
Wriggling and writhing, bleeding all over the floor,
And my feline friend just sits there
*   and looks at me with pride;*
"For Goodness sake Tommy! Take that thing outside!"

To date we've had a sparrow, a blue tit and a vole,
A rather irksome rat and a politely inconvenienced mole.
You see, he never ever eats them, to him it's just a game –
And how the little field mice laugh as
*   they are gruesomely maimed.*

He even gave us a frog once who – you've guessed it -
*   was hopping mad.*
Yes, I hear you groan at the joke, but otherwise it's so sad.
The house is a menagerie, it's like the British Museum.
But next to be stuffed is that blinking cat the next time
*   I happen to see him.*

Can't he bring me something I want or something I can use?
What can I do with a half-dead shrew squeaking
*   me the blues?*
Why can't he get the paper or bring me in the post?

*He just sits at my feet with next door's fish and has
   the nerve to boast.*

*So, Tommy, I know it's only nature, I know it's
   what you do,
But for goodness sake Tommy, do it somewhere else —
   or I'll do nature to you.*

The children laughed aloud as Dai performed his poem. For a moment time seemed to stop. Life was frozen. It was as though he was looking back on a photograph of a fondly remembered period in his past. He looked around the room and saw faces glowing with laughter, children bent doubled, rolling around to a harmony of giggles and chuckles, and the morning sun streaming through the windows. In the centre of the picture was a familiar little face; Ieuan. He was not laughing, rather he was smiling proudly as the children around him were possessed by hilarity and merriment. His face beamed, radiating pride and love for his father. Then as quickly as the photograph had a chance to form in Dai's mind, it disappeared into the cruel realms of reality. A quick blink was all it took to realize that Ieuan was not there at all, just in his memory. As the children continued to roll around on the floor in pure delight, Dai's world fell apart once more. The smile fell from his face, collapsing like the dreams he once had.

The sound of Bronnie calling the children to order pulled Dai out of his suspended animation. He felt a tap on his leg.

'When I grow up I want to be like you,' stated little Chloe.

'Thank you, young lady,' replied Dai with the softest of smiles. He was moved, almost the point of tears, but after a deep breath managed to keep his emotions in check. 'And when I grow young I want to be just like you, because you are very kind and polite.'

The girl smiled and took her place once again on the carpet. Dai looked around the classroom and reveled in the children's love and adoration and there, at the back of the class, smiling most proud of all, was little Hemi. Dai had never seen such happiness in one place, not since the day he first set eyes on his son.

Following the success of the ad hoc English session, Dai sat in the staffroom at break-time where he met Bronnie's colleagues and indulged in a well-earned cup of tea. While engaged in some polite, but idle conversation with George his eyes drifted toward the staffroom window. Outside he watched as Hemi climbed across the monkey bars in the playground and a smile spread over his face as he watched the boy holding on tightly to the roundabout and laughing with the other children. He giggled as the boy twisted and contorted his slender body around the climbing apparatus. The child seemed to delight in running around the playground dodging the other children and laughing continuously. However, the mood of his gaze changed when he caught sight of the imposing Ruru, sweeping in the yard. He seemed just as fearsome as he had when they had collided in the supermarket. Dai took a sip of his tea to calm him down.

Following his beverage, Dai decided to walk home to the Havelock house. Perhaps a little exercise and fresh air would do him some good. As he headed over the bridge, the familiar voice of Hemi called out to him to wait. The little boy ran and caught up with him.

'What are you doing out of school?' asked Dai.

'Doctor's.'

'Why?' pressed Dai. 'What's wrong?'

'Nothing, just a check up.' The subject was changed. 'When did you know you wanted to be a writer?'

'Why do you ask?' Dai was surprised by the boy's interest. 'I thought you said that books were boring.'

'Most of them are.'

Dai huffed. 'And I suppose you are talking from a whole seven years of life experience?'

'How old were you?'

A big sigh and a scratch of the head. 'About eight, I think,' said Dai.

Hemi began to walk backwards in front of Dai. 'I really liked your poems.'

'Thanks.'

'They were funny.'

'Would you like to be a writer?' asked Dai.

'Don't know!' He shrugged his skinny shoulders. 'I don't know if I'd be any good at it.'

'You don't know until you try.'

'Anyway they're not much use, are they?'

'What do you mean?' asked Dai.

'Well, it's not really a job is it?' Dai laughed to disguise the mild offence he had taken. 'You know what I mean.'

'No, not really.'

'Well, you can't mend anything with a poem, can you? You can't make anyone better with a story. You can't make anything with a book.'

'Oh, I don't know,' said Dai, 'I hear some people can make a good door wedge from my books?'

'What?' Hemi looked confused.

'Joke.' Still nothing from Hemi. 'Never mind. The point is, you don't have to make something with your hands, you can create something with your heart.'

'What do you mean?'

'Well, you can tell stories to make people think about the way they are feeling, or you tell stories to stop people thinking. Sometimes we just need to escape this world. And as for making people better... well, that's why I write.'

'To make people better?'

'To make myself better.' The boy, once again was perplexed. 'When I feel sad, when I feel lonely... I write. There was a man called C.S Lewis...'

'The Lion, The Witch and The Wardrobe?' Hemi interrupted.

'Yes, that's the chap.'

'Well, he once said, "we read to know we are not alone." I'm never alone when I write. There's always a crazy bunch of characters around. And they do exactly what I tell them to do!'

'I suppose.'

'Some people have had their lives saved by stories.'

The boy was instantly dismissive. 'Rubbish!'

'It's true!'

'No it is not,' smiled Hemi, 'you liar.'

'Scheherazade!'

'Bless you!'

'No, Scheherazade.' He clipped the boy's ear playfully. 'She told stories to save her own life.'

'Well, go on then!'

'A king of Persia was devastated when he found out his wife had been unfaithful to him. He was angry, livid, consumed with madness. To take revenge on womankind he would marry a woman, take her to bed, have his wicked way and then, in the morning…' he drew an invisible line across his throat, 'cut her head off.'

'Errr!' said Hemi.

'Then one day he met Scheherazade and thought he would do the same thing to her. However, that night she started to tell him one of the many stories she had learned as a child, but told the king that she would finish it the next day. The king was so intrigued by the story that he spared her life in order to hear the rest of the tale the following day. And so it went on. She told him a new story every day, over a thousand and one nights and during that time the king let go of his anger and his pain. He fell in love with her.'

'Wow.'

'A Thousand and One Arabian Nights. I'll lend you the book.'

'Dad never really like to read. He's never really read books to me.'

'That's a shame.'

'No, he used to sing to me.'

'Oh, well I imagine that was nice.'

'He's got a good voice, my Dad,' he said proudly. 'I used to have trouble sleeping. I used to be really scared of the dark. I'm okay now though. Anyway, when I was scared, Dad would sing.'

'What did he sing?' asked Dai.

'Pokarekare Ana, but my favourite was Hine E Hine. When I was five, I had a bad dream. It was Halloween and I dreamed I was being chased by a big skeleton. I woke up screaming and Dad gave me a hug for a while and sang that song.'

'How does it go?' asked a curious Dai.

'You want me to sing it?'

'Yes, why not?'

'I can't sing.'

'Oh, come on,' said Dai, 'you can't be any worse that my wife.'

Hemi smiled, 'Oh, okay.'

> *E Tanagi ana koe*
> *Hine e hine*
> *Kua ngenge an koe*
> *Hine e hine*
> *Kati to pouri ra*
> *Noho I te Aroha*
> *Te ngakau o te Matua*
> *Hine e hine*

Dai smiled at Hemi, 'Very nice!' he said, 'Very nice indeed. You were right about one thing you know.'

'What was that?' asked Hemi.

'You really can't sing.'

'Hey!' protested Hemi, punching Dai playfully on the arm.

The two continued to walk home together, over the river and up the long, winding road which snaked its way up the hillside. Dai recalled fond memories of walking Ieuan home from school, hearing about his day and finding out what he had learned in class. Then his memory travelled even further, back to his own childhood, walking home with his own school friends – "Big Ears" Benji, Spencer Gray and Matty Poole. He remembered how they were careful not to step on the cracks in the pavement for fear of one day marrying Smelly – or Sarah Small as she was known on the register. In Hemi he had found an unlikely friend who had the uncanny knack of being so profound without ever knowing it.

They both arrived at The Havelock house and Dai told Hemi to wait outside for a moment. While Dai went inside the house, Hemi looked through the windows into the living room. He saw how neat and ordered the place was and when Dai finally emerged, passed comment.

'You don't have children do you?'

Dai was taken aback. 'Why do you say that?'

'Your house is so tidy. My Dad says that once you have kids, you have to get used to living in a mess.'

Dai suddenly felt a compulsion to tell the little boy all about Ieuan. It seemed the greatest gift he could give, the most profound sign of their growing friendship.

'No, I don't have any…' He hesitated.

'Any what?'

Dai wondered if telling about Ieuan would be in Hemi's interest or in his own. To tell one so young about something so tragic would, he thought, be unfair.

'I don't have any room for children. It's only a small house.'

'D'you think you'll have children one day?' asked Hemi innocently.

'Well...' Dai changed the subject and gave Hemi the book he had brought from inside. 'Here you are.'

'Thanks,' he took the book and looked at the front cover. 'A Thousand and One Arabian Nights.'

'Enjoy! I'll see you later.'

Hemi headed off down the garden to the path that would lead him back down the hillside, reading as he walked. His attention was so absorbed that he walked straight into the washing line, much to the amusement of Dai. He turned back to see if his friend had noticed and smiled through an embarrassed blush.

'Silly sod!'

Later that afternoon, Dai sat beneath the Havelock house and despite his euphoria following the morning's successful meeting with the children at the School, still had no idea what he would write. Hemi came bounding, as usual from the bushes at the bottom of the garden.

'Hi Dai.'

'Hiya Hemi,' he looked at his watch, 'Good grief, you must have run all the way up that hill.'

'I'm the fastest in my class,' he claimed with a smile of self-satisfaction. Then he paused. 'Well, apart from Jim, he's a little bit faster than me... and Joanna... and Maaka... and possibly Hayden... Austin is definitely faster than me, but that's only because he is bigger than me.'

'Can you actually run?' asked Dai sarcastically.

'Yeah, but I can't swim.' He mimed a front crawl. 'I don't like the water.'

'Why?'

'Dad says it's just one of those things. It scares me.'

Dai smiled warmly at the boy. 'There's nothing to be afraid of, Hemi.'

'Dad says we're all afraid of something.'

'Yes, I suppose so.'

'What are you afraid of Dai?'

He took a moment to think. 'Well I suppose I have always been afraid of death. But I haven't felt it as much recently.' He smiled. 'Its inevitability…' he stopped as the boy struggled with Dai's choice of words and rephrased. 'The fact that I knew we were all going to die used to terrify me. I wouldn't be able to sleep at night. Now it doesn't frighten me as much. Anyway we're all treading the road to Hinenuitepo.'

Hemi smiled. 'You remembered the story.'

'Yes, what made you tell me that story?'

'It was a story my Dad used to tell me.'

Dai sat back in his chair. 'What do you do when someone dies? I mean the Maori. How do they deal with death?'

'You mean the Tangihanga.'

'What's that?' asked Dai.

'That's how we say goodbye to someone when they die.'

'Tell me.'

'Can I have the storyteller's chair?' Hemi said with a disarming smile.

Dai smiled at the boy admiring his cheekiness. Hemi took his place in the chair and Dai, once again, took his place on the grass before him.

'We usually just call it the tangi. It goes on for three days at the marae.'

'The marae?' interrupted Dai.

'That's where we live.'

'Oh, I see.'

The boy continued. 'It's where we help the whanau pani.' Dai looked for a translation. 'That's the family. The family who have lost someone. We do what we can to help them when they're sad. All the way through the tangi the body is never alone. There's always someone with them. All the family and friends get together. Sometimes people you hardly ever see come to say farewell. It's where people can come and say goodbye to the person one last time. And it's not just crying. We try to remember funny things about them as well. In our marae we have a Po Whakangakau on the final night where we sing, tell stories and jokes before we say goodbye to the body.'

'Then?' asked Dai.

'Then that is it.'

'It sounds much more fun than our funerals.'

'Why?' asked Hemi, swinging his legs from the storyteller's chair.

'Well, the priest tells us that we are all there to celebrate the life of the loved one, but the organ plays miserable music and he speaks in the most miserable voice. And then we have to listen to a complete stranger talk to us about our loved one. He tells us all the things we already knew; that the child was kind, happy, funny, clever...'

'Child?' interrupted Hemi.

'What?'

'You said, "child."'

'Did I?' Dai paused for a moment. 'Well, whoever it is, the point is that you seem to have a much more realistic and positive idea of death.'

Another awkward moment followed. Dai was in danger of remembering and Hemi, so Dai thought, was too young for such moroseness.

'Anyway,' said Dai with a change of tone, 'it's a nice hot day. You need to learn to swim.'

'No, I don't want to, I don't like…' Hemi's protests were cut short.

'Nonsense! I will help you.' Dai took off his t-shirt to reveal his white, bare chest.

'But I don't want to…'

'Come on! Let's go!'

'Dai! I don't want to!' shouted Hemi.

Dai was shocked out of his enthusiasm and felt guilt consume him as Hemi started to cry.

'It's okay, Hemi.' He put his hand on the boy's shoulder. 'Okay, let's just go wading. I'm sorry. I didn't mean to upset you.'

'I told you I was scared of the water,' said Hemi through his tears.

'I know, I really am sorry.'

'We'll just paddle?'

'Yes, I promise.' He ruffled the boy's hair softly. 'Come on. You live by the water don't you?'

'Yeah.' He wiped a tear away with the back of his hand, leaving a dirty streak, which stretched from the corner of his eye to his hairline.

'Show me your house, it would give me a chance to meet your Dad.'

'He's probably not there.'

'Why not?'

'Because. He's probably out again.' Dai refused the temptation to ask any more questions, yet he wondered why a little boy would be left alone so often. 'Anyway, it's this way.'

Hemi led the way through the bushes at the end of the garden, over the waist-high wooden fence and down through a narrow path, which weaved through the forest that blanketed the hillside. The path seemed to go on forever, yet the walk was pleasant. The sweet scent of flax flowers wafted through the air, the sound of the tui calling echoed through the canopy above and as they descended further on down the hillside. Dai could hear the sound of wavelets kissing the shoreline. Finally, they came to a clearing by the water's edge and there in view was a small wooden house. The building was in a state of disrepair. Paint was flaking off the outside walls and the yard outside was overgrown.

'This is your house?' asked Dai.

'Yeah, Dad's not here.'

'How d'you know?'

'The boat's not here,' he headed round to the back of the house. 'Come on, I'll show you my room.'

'Okay.' Dai was confused. 'Why don't you go through the front door?'

'I don't have a key,' he said, lifting a window open. 'So I climb through the window. You coming in?'

'The last time I crawled in through an unlocked window I was sixteen. It was the newsagents. I was trying to get hold of some dirty magazines. I was given a caution from the police. I think I'll look from here.'

Hemi climbed through the window and into his bedroom, which like many a young boy's room was a mess. There were toys scattered around the floor, a fishing rod leant up in the corner and painted pictures on the wall.

'Did you paint those?' asked Dai.

'Yeah,' he replied. 'Did them at school.'

There was a signed picture of Kiwi rugby legend Jonah Lomu framed on the bedside.

'Wow! Did you meet him?' asked Dai.

'No, my Dad met him.'

'Really!'

'Yeah, Dad once played against him in a charity match.'

Dai was impressed. 'Wow! Your Dad must be a good player.'

'Used to be.' Hemi picked up a model plane and flew it around the room, complete with sound effects. 'He stopped playing years ago.'

'I see.'

'So do you like my room?'

'It's...'

'What?' asked Hemi.

'It's... It's just as a boy's bedroom should be.' Hemi smiled. 'Right, let's get our feet wet, shall we?'

'You promise we're just paddling?'

'I promise.'

Hemi climbed back out of the window and held Dai's hand nervously. Dai led them to the front of the house, to the edge of the overgrown lawn where it met the shoreline. They walked along the line of the shore to where a long boat launch protruded out into deeper water. A small fishing boat, big enough only for two was moored to the launch by a frayed yet substantial rope. The paddle of the oars could be seen poking out the top of the boat. Dai could see from Hemi's brow that he was not comfortable here. Nevertheless he persisted in Hemi's best interest.

'Are you ready for a dip?'

'The boy hesitated. 'Um… Do you know how to skate?'

'I'm sorry?' asked Dai.

'Do you skate?'

'Well, I tried many years ago but I never could stand up in the boots. I kept falling on my arse.'

'No!' laughed Hemi. 'Not ice-skating.'

Hemi bent down and picked up a thin, flat stone from his feet, brushed off the excess sand and smoothed it on his shorts, before hurling it low, long and fast into the water. The stone skipped once, twice, three, then four times along the surface of the water until it disappeared for another million years or so beneath the waves.

'Stones!'

'Oh!' said Dai. 'We call it skimming.'

'You any good?'

A smug grin. 'I think seven is my record.'

'Go on then,' said Hemi.

'Well, let me see what we have down here.' Dai fumbled around among the stones and pebbles at his feet and came upon another flat missile. He rubbed the stone in his groin, like a cricketer polishing the seam, then picked up a leaf and watched it fall to assess the wind direction. He went one step further and licked his index finger and held it comically in the air much to the amusement of Hemi.

'Are you going to throw that or what?'

'I have to assess the conditions, young man. I have to determine a great many things before throwing. You can't just launch it willy-nilly into the water. That's why you are a mere four bouncer, where as I am a sevener. You have to consider the weight of the stone, the surface of the stone, the wind direction, atmospherics, the angle of entry, the wetness of the water, time of the month...'

'Dai...' said Hemi through his laughter.

'What?'

'Throw the stone!'

Dai hurled the stone as hard and as fast as he could and watched it crash with a loud splosh into the first wave it hit.

'Don't say a word!' said Dai.

Hemi then casually picked up a stone and, without ceremony, skimmed it eight times on the surface of the water.

'I think that beats your record.'

Dai tried to keep a straight face but quickly succumbed to laughter.

'Anyway,' he said after a moment or two, 'you changed the subject.'

Dai removed his shoes and told Hemi to take off his sandals, which he did reluctantly. He reached out his hand and waited for Hemi to take hold. After a few nervous breaths, Hemi reached out his hand and gripped tightly. A flash of memory came to Dai and for one second he recalled Ieuan's little hand hold tightly around two of his fingers as they walked through the main street in Penarth to do the shopping. The memory was blinked away and Dai did his best to reassure Hemi.

'Okay,' he said softly, 'I have your hand, nothing is going to happen to you.'

'You won't let go?'

'I won't let go, I'm your friend.' Hemi smiled for a second. 'I promise.'

One step, then two, then three. After a minute or so Dai had safely negotiated them both knee-deep into the Pelorus Sounds. Between steps Hemi was motionless. The only movement came from the occasional shudder which ran through his body. Dai could feel each little tremor conduct through his own body. The chill of the gentle wavelets was refreshing beneath the afternoon sun and Dai wanted nothing more than to dive head first into to the water.

'Do you want to go in any further?' asked Dai.

'No, can I stay here?' he replied.

'Yes, that's fine.'

The two unlikely friends stood hand in hand in the shallows near Havelock, looking out over the water in complete peace and contentment. Not a word was shared for a moment. They were both happy in the silence.

'I want to go back now.'

Dai turned to Hemi and smiled. 'Okay.'

When they had made it to the shore Dai told Hemi to wait for a moment or two while he went into the water for a swim. The boy agreed and Dai ran into the water screaming wildly, much to the delight of Hemi, and dived beneath the waves. Dai had always loved the water and for a moment he was taken back to his own childhood where he would jump and splash and drag his arm in circles along the surface of the water to make his own waves. Hemi laughed as Dai made a delightful idiot of himself. Then, as high spirits consumed him, Dai took a deep breath and pretended to be dragged under the water. Once again Hemi laughed with glee.

'Dai!' he called behind his giggles.

Dai, holding his breath under the water, kept himself hidden to Hemi, but soon the laughter began to fade.

'Okay,' said Hemi, 'I know you're in there.'

Nothing.

'Dai! Dai! Come out now.' Hemi's voice became more concerned. He scanned the water which by now was as still as a lily pond. He looked for signs of activity on the water, some waves or some bubbles perhaps. He took a tentative step into the water to look closer as the fear started to consume him. By now nearly a minute had past without sign of Dai. The hairs on his stick-thin arms began to stand on end and his insides began to turn over and over. He screamed at the top of his lungs.

'DAI!'

At that moment Dai leapt out of the water with a huge intake of air. The sound of his massive inhalation, and the spray from the water shattered the silence of the forest. Bird calls erupted, as did the clatter of flapping wings as pigeons and tuis flew into the sky in fright. Dai wiped the salty water from his eyes and smiled at Hemi, seeking his approval. Yet the boy's face was fierce although brimming with tears. He stood for a moment, shaking, shuddering, and shimmering like the ripples drifting away from Dai after his emergence from the shallows.

'What's wrong?' asked Dai.
'That wasn't funny.'
'Oh, come on. I was just fooling around.'
'I'm going inside.'
Dai watched the little boy turn around and walk back towards his house, his confident and quirky swagger was gone. Dai was perplexed.

10. FURY, FIRE AND STARS

A thunderstorm had just passed. The air, which had been hot and oppressive for the last two days, was now rich with the aroma of hot, damp soil. The heat was still trapped beneath the fern leaves which grew behind the school grounds. As the sun crept out once again, the vapours could be seen drifting up off the playground floor and up to the sky. Bronnie looked out of Mrs Anders' office and watched as the large, black clouds gave way to perfect blue sky. She waited anxiously for a while before Anders finally entered with the angry looking figure of Mrs Stone following close behind. Anders invited Harry's mother to sit at a round meeting table with Bronnie. She sat with her arms folded and stared defiantly at both staff in turn. Anders tried to lighten the situation.

'Right Mrs Stone,' she said in her usual insincere voice, 'could I interest you in a cup of tea?'

'No.'

'How about a coffee?'

'No.'

'Would you like a drink of water?' she persisted. 'Something cold?'

'I would like to know why I am here.' She shuffled uncomfortably in her chair. 'I have lots to do.'

'Well, hopefully this won't take too long to sort out.'

'Sort what out?' said Stone, who was becoming increasingly annoyed. 'Can someone just tell me why I am here please?'

Mrs Anders continued to skirt around the issue. 'Well, I uh…'

'Where did Harry get those bruises?' said Bronnie, abruptly, sitting forward in her chair.

Anders closed her eyes and tried to imagine that Bronnie hadn't opened her mouth.

'I beg your pardon,' said Mrs Stone.

Anders tried to calm the situation with a softening tone, 'It's just that…'

'You heard me?' said Bronnie. 'Where did Harry get his bruises? And how?'

'What on earth are you talking about?'

'You know damn well what I'm talking about.'

'Ladies,' said Mrs Anders, 'Let's just calm things down a little, shall we?'

'I will do no such thing.' Mrs Stone stood up furiously. 'I'm not going to sit here and listen to you accuse me of…'

'Mrs Stone please sit down, nobody is accusing anybody of anything.' Anders successfully defused the situation for a moment. Mrs Stone returned to her seat. 'However, we are concerned about Harry.'

'I haven't touched him,' insisted Mrs Stone.

'Then how did he get those marks?' asked Bronnie.

'What marks?'

'The bruises on his arms, the marks beneath his collar line, the abrasions beneath his hair line.'

'I haven't seen any marks at all.'

Bronnie rolled her eyes. 'You must be joking.'

'Ladies, please!' shouted Anders.

Bronnie and Mrs Stone stared each other squarely in the eye, each refusing to be the one to look away first.

'Is everything okay at home Mrs Stone?' asked Anders.

'Yes. Harry and I are fine.'

'That's not the way we are seeing things here, I'm afraid,' said Mrs Anders.

'Why?'

'He's becoming more and more withdrawn,' replied Bronnie. 'He doesn't speak to anyone, he doesn't play with anyone. He stands alone at break time.'

'And what would you know about it?' said Mrs Stone, squinting her eyes at Bronnie. 'You're not even his teacher.'

'I know enough to realize that there is something wrong with the boy,' Bronnie squinted back, 'which is more than you seem to know.'

'How dare you!' erupted Mrs Stone. 'Anyway, what are you doing with your hands all over my son? I could call the police.'

'Please do!' insisted Bronnie.

'For goodness sake ladies,' interrupted Mrs Anders, 'nobody is calling the police. We just need to ensure that Harry is safe and well. Mrs Stone, where is Harry's father?'

'I don't know.'

Mrs Anders leaned forward and rested her arms on the table while Bronnie chewed her fingernails.

'I don't understand,' said Mrs Anders.

'Harry's father left shortly after he was born.'

'And he has no contact with Harry at all?' the Head continued.

'None,' said Mrs Stone abruptly. 'It's just Harry and me.'

'And what about…'

Mrs Stone cut the Headmistress short. 'Look there's nothing wrong with Harry and I haven't got time to sit here and discuss this crap with you. Just keep your noses out of our business and leave us alone. In the meantime, you can expect a letter to your governors and the education authorities. Now leave us alone.'

Mrs Stone rose swiftly and stormed out of the office, leaving Bronnie unconvinced and Mrs Anders livid with Bronnie. The Head shut the door and sighed angrily.

'What on earth was all that about?'

'I tell you! There is something going on there. You saw how defensive she was then.'

'Good grief,' Mrs Anders was enraged. 'Of course she was defensive! Wouldn't you be defensive is someone accused you of being a child-beater? For Christ's sake!'

'You have to get that child out of her care,' insisted Bronnie.

'On what grounds?' Mrs Anders slammed her hands down on the table, startling Bronnie. 'Where's the evidence?'

'Just look at the boy's body for goodness sake. Look at the marks.'

'How do you know he got them from her?'

Bronnie had no answer. Her anger and her fears for Harry were suddenly so concentrated, so intense, that she was unable to speak.

'I suggest you go back to your class while I try to speak to the governors before Mrs Stone and undo some of the damage you have done.'

That evening Bronnie and Dai sat in well-mannered chit-chat. The conversation over dinner was polite yet unremarkable. Dai had still to mention Hemi and Bronnie continued to keep quiet about the ongoing saga with Harry. Yet the unspoken secrets seemed to drift around the house and created an air of mistrust and suspicion. More concerning however, was the continued silence on the subject of Ieuan. Both did their best not to bring up their lost son in discourse for fear of reliving even the smallest moment of grief. As such, the house continued to be a silent, stilted home of dull, trivial and inconsequential conversation.

Dai had not seen Hemi since his joke had backfired in the shallows near his house. He was concerned. In the short time that Dai had known Hemi, he had begun to develop the most unlikely of friendships, one that was simple yet sincere. While Bronnie set to work on a two-foot tower of marking which would see her through until bedtime, Dai stepped outside. He sat beneath the house and waited for Hemi's familiar rustle in the bushes at the bottom of the garden. By the time it became clear that Hemi was not coming, the sun had set beneath the hills and Dai resolved to find his little friend.

Playing Beneath the Havelock House

Dai followed the path through the ferns to the sound of the dusk chorus and the gently crescendoing tones of the nearing waves. Soon he spied the little house by the river and quietly he crept up to Hemi's window. He looked inside and saw the toys still scattered around the room but the boy was nowhere to be seen. He tapped lightly on the window and called softly for Hemi. Nothing.

By now the sun had well and truly set and night was drawing swiftly upon Havelock. The trees and bushes cast the house into further darkness. Dai waited around the house for a while but there was no sign of Hemi. He called out to his friend once more but the only response came from a startled possum from beneath a host of ferns.

Before Dai could call again the clattering sound of a motor boat coming could be heard. The noise became louder and closer, then stopped. Dai poked his head around the side of the house and saw the shadow of a small boat, big enough only for two, being moored to the boat launch by a tall man. Dai squinted his eyes but couldn't see a face. He assumed it was Hemi's father and he would not take kindly to a stranger snooping around his house. But where was Hemi?

Dai kept himself hidden behind the house. He watched as the man made his way toward the house with a large metal tin. His heavy steps could be heard clumping down the wooden boat launch like the thundering sound of a giant in a fairy story. Even from a safe distance, Dai felt anything but safe. His heart began to race and he looked behind him to check his escape route back home, but the compulsion to know more was overwhelming. The man made his way to the front door while Dai headed surreptitiously to Hemi's window at the back of the house. He sat down beneath the window ledge and listened to the sound of doors banging and squeaking within the rickety old building. He felt the blood cascade through his veins and could hear his pulse pound in his ears. Thud! Thud! Thud! Then there was a silence. With the stillness came fear, then curiosity. Dai swallowed hard and slowly turned his head to look into Hemi's window. His heart almost burst as he saw the towering man standing with his back to the window in Hemi's room looking at the toys on the floor. Dai pulled his head in quickly and tried desperately to control his breathing. He feared that each and every breath would disturb the man and expose him. He sat motionless beneath the window as the seconds turned to minutes before finally hearing the slam of a door close by. He remained where he was, this time successfully holding his curiosity at bay, until he heard the font door shut. Dai headed to the side of the house and hid down in the overgrown grass between the walls and the corrugated iron curves of a cylindrical water tank. In the darkness he could just see the man pull out a sofa, then a mattress, then, one by one, a small dining room table and chairs and placed them, without ceremony, on a faded patch of grass between the front of the house and the water's edge. Then as the clouds gathered above, blocking out the meager light from the rising moon, Dai heard the glugging sound of fluids being poured hastily out of the metal tin. Then, in the lightless Sounds, he watched as the man lit a match and tossed it on to the pile of furniture, sending the whole thing up in flames. Dai was startled and as he stepped in fear he tripped over a length of hosing and fell to the ground. The man was startled.

'Who's there?' he said.

Dai stumbled to his feet and ran as fast as he could back into the forest, stumbling and tripping at almost every step. He looked behind to see if the man was following him, but in the pitch black he could not be sure. His heart leapt out of his chest with every beat and the fear, which accompanied each inhalation and exhalation, rattled his vocal chords to a nervous moan. As the night blanketed Pelorus Sounds all Dai could think to do was run.

The possums scattered off the lawn as Dai stumbled, out of breath, sweating, back into his garden. He slumped down into his chair as the clouds gave way to moonlight. He looked up at the sky, his heart still racing in his chest to a metronomic thud, thud, thud, and saw the stars emerge one by one. As he recovered his breathing he looked into the cosmos, to the great expanse of space, matter and time and allowed his heart to speak to him.

A picture emerged, one he had seen before. Now the stars in the sky were clear as he looked through the lens of Ieuan's telescope on Christmas evening. New worlds and old heavens presented themselves as he squinted through the eyepiece.

'What can you see, Daddy?' said Ieuan's gentle voice.

'Everything, buddy. Everything.' The little boy smiled. 'It's huge.'

As he scanned the night sky a bolt of realization struck him like lightening. Then a moment of existential perception washed over him as gently as the winter breeze weaving through the sky outside the window.

'There is more than this,' he whispered to himself, 'more than now, more than forever.'

Only weeks after that night behind the telescope, doctors diagnosed Ieuan's leukemia, and those words were lost.

Dai returned to the present and, for the first time since he held his son's hand as the heat drained from it in those final hours, he felt the radiance of Ieuan's love once more. He couldn't understand it, but he could feel it. He knew it wasn't God; why, he thought, would an all powerful deity or celestial being take his son only to give him back? This was beyond God. He imagined for a moment following the source of his feelings, through time and space, through the stars, beyond the planets, left at the supernova, right at the hurtling comet, straight on through the winding wormhole and straight back to that part of his heart which he thought had died. He felt warmth at his side and looked to find its source. There was nothing there, yet still he reached out his hand and felt it move through the heat. He stood up slowly, doing his best to keep one hand on the source of the heat and as he steadied himself in the darkness, felt the warmth with his other hand. The heat source seemed to stop, just above his waist height. He knelt down gently and moved his hands slowly and lovingly through the warmth in front of him. His hand twisted and turned as though swimming through the night air. He breathed the warmth into his lungs and into his heart and finally his heart was filled with love once more.

'Ieuan,' he said, 'I miss you buddy, I miss you so much.'

The tears began to fall from his eyes and run softly through the lines in his face and as they collected at tips on his nose, they formed into droplets which glistened in the moonlight. Yet within the tears he felt the healing begin. And as his hands drifted through the warmth, he heard a rustle at the bottom of the garden. He leapt to his feet and moved quickly to the edge of the lawn where the grass met the foliage.

'Hemi?' he called wiping his eyes. 'Hemi is that you?'

The sound of the rustling became softer and more distant and Dai assumed that the noise could be attributed to the wandering possums. Then, as he headed for the steps which would lead him inside into the arms of Bronnie, he heard a cheeky voice and a mischievous laughter.

'See you later Pākehā.'

'Where are you?' Dai smiled and allowed himself a little chuckle. He made his way up the steps to the back door and smiled again. 'Little turd!'

Before he headed into the house he cleared his face so as to hide any signs of his crying from Bronnie before whispering into the darkness.

'See you tomorrow.'

11. TRUST AND TRUTHS

The children made their way into the assembly hall in not-so-silent silence, much to the dismay of Mrs Anders who always insisted on the children entering without making a sound. It was Bronnie's turn to deliver her talk to the school. She stood at the front of the hall while the children shuffled in and could feel Mrs Anders eyes staring at her from the side of the hall. She didn't need to look to see if she was there, she could feel the Headteacher's uneasy presence all around her. Bronnie was in no doubt that things would soon become even more uncomfortable by the time the assembly was done.

'Okay, boys and girls, could you look this way please?' she asked with nervous authority.

The children looked attentively and Bronnie waited for the chatty din to soften to a series of whispers.

'I want to talk to you about something important, so it is very important that you listen really carefully.' The whispers finally descended into silence. 'Who can you trust?'

Bronnie left a pregnant pause. The children looked at each other, they looked at their hands, they looked at their fingernails, but all were silent.

'It's a tricky one, isn't it? Who can you trust?' she scanned the hall. 'Tommy, who do you trust?'

The little curly-haired boy thought for a moment. Bronnie waited patiently for a response.

'I would trust a policeman, Miss,' he said.

'A policeman.'

'Yes, Miss.'

'I see.' Bronnie turned to the other side of the hall. 'What about you Molly? Who do you trust?'

The girl played with her long black hair for a while. Once again Bronnie afforded the little girl the courtesy of thinking time. While Molly considered her answer Bronnie caught the piercing eyes of Mrs Anders and knew that trouble would lie ahead.

'I trust my ancestors, Miss.'

'Why is that?' asked Bronnie.

'Because they are always looking out for us.'

'Okay.'

'What about your family?' said Bronnie addressing the whole school again. 'We all trust our family, don't we?'

Bronnie searched out the eyes of little Harry Stone. She found him, head down, at the end of one of the uneven rows of children. Her eyes implored him to look up yet his gaze was fixed on is lap.

'Don't we? We trust our brothers and our sisters, surely? And of course we trust our fathers.' She moved to the end of the row and hovered in front of Harry. 'What about our mothers? We trust them don't we?'

Awkwardly, Mrs Anders interrupted.

'Mrs Ifans, could I just have a quick word with you, please?'

Bronnie ignored the Headteacher.

'What happens when you find that you can't trust those closest to you? What do you do when you can't trust those you should trust the most? You see, sometimes we can be hurt by the very people who love us. And sometimes we don't want to tell anyone about it because we love them too.'

'Mrs Ifans,' said the squirming Anders, 'I really must insist.'

'You can all trust your teacher. You see, each of you here is a miracle. You are a life. You have a life and it is your right to be… cared for… worried about… loved.'

Mrs Anders was about to step up when the greying Mrs Simpson, placed her hand on the Headteacher's shoulder, halted her advance and whispered in her ear.

'You'll make things worse,' said Simpson, 'Don't cause a scene.'

Bronnie continued. 'You have the right to be loved. If you are not… cared for by those who should care for you most, you must find someone else you can trust. To love a child is the greatest privilege that any adult can have.' Bronnie looked up to the rest of the school once more as a tear began to well in her eye. 'To harm a child is the greatest sin. You are so precious. I had a little boy…'

Bronnie scanned the hall of children, confused by the profundity of her words and saw Ieuan sitting cross-legged on the wooden floor. Her gaze was fixed for a moment, but with a blink he was taken once more. As his vision disappeared she felt the grief as deeply as the day he died. She felt a pain in her chest which descended to the pit of her stomach and she noticed the tingles all around her body, as if a million needles were piercing her skin at the same time. Her stance became unsteady and the children began to whisper once again as they saw their teacher all but collapse in front of them.

'I had a little boy... A very... special little boy... he... he...'

Just as the words failed her, a little child from the reception stood up and moved toward Bronnie. The little boy, Arana, with transfer Maori tattoos on his slender arms, took Bronnie by the hand and without saying anything stood at her side. Bronnie looked down at the boy and held his hand tighter. She felt the purest love run back into her veins, like a transfusion of happiness. Arana had sucked the poison from her wound and with the softest and tiniest of hands kissed and cleansed the wound.

'His name was Ieuan. He was my little boy. He...' She took the deepest breath, '...he died.'

The tears flowed freely, released like the most colourful bird from the darkest cage. The warmth of her tears and Arana's hand brought comfort to Bronnie and the gentle admission of Ieuan's death brought the sweetest of smiles to her face. She bent down and picked Arana up and embraced him with all the love she had. As the tears fell another child rose to comfort her and hold her other hand, then another child, and another, and another until within a moment all of the children in the little school had descended upon her and encircled her with the simple love that only children seem to be able to offer. As the children gathered round her, Bronnie thought about the money she had spent on therapists, the time she had spent talking to well-meaning relatives, days reliving the words of the priest at the Ieuan's funeral and marveled that consolation should come at the hands of one so young. Although a teacher of children for many years, it was now her turn to learn from her pupils. What a beautiful lesson it was.

Thankfully there were no repercussions of the talk of trust in the assembly, yet neither was there any sympathy from Mrs Anders toward Bronnie. As Bronnie headed for her car that evening, she spotted a football left in the middle of the playground. She placed her box-full of marking into the back of the car and returned to the playground to retrieve the football and put it in its proper place. The sports shed was at the back of the school in the corner of the playing field. As she headed across the field she thought about what had happened that day. She felt as though the weight of her grief had been lightened. She knew it would never leave her, but she could see the first glimmers of hope for the future on the horizon. Nearing the shed, she began to hear noises. At first they were almost inaudible, but slowly they became a little louder. She stopped for a while to check the source of the sound, looking around the open field for clues. Nothing. Slowly she moved step by careful step toward the shed and heard the familiar sound of a child crying. Something felt uncomfortable. She crept up to the shed and swallowed hard, fearing what she might find. Finally, she came upon the shed and heard more quiet whimpers from inside. She looked through the window and saw Harry sitting slumped on the floor delivering blows to his body with his own hands. She watched as the little boy punched his ribs as hard as he could, following each pounding blow with restrained cries. He followed the blows to his body with thumps to his head. Bronnie watched in horror as Harry continued to abuse his tiny body, wanting to stop him, but she was paralysed with sadness and disbelief. However, after a harrowing moment or two she opened the shed door. Harry recoiled then retreated into the corner, and tried to disappear into the darkness.

'It's okay Harry.'

The boy had nowhere to run, but still tried to back further into the wooden panels of the shed.

'Its okay, I'm here.' She reached out her slender hand to the boy who was now trembling from head to toe. 'I'm here to help. I want to help you.'

He began to cry. Each shake and shudder forced the tears into a zig-zag pattern down his pale cheeks.

'Nobody can help,' he said.

'Why not?'

'Because there's nothing that anyone can do.'

Bronnie hesitated while she searched for something to say; something which might alleviate the boy's pain.

'Nobody has hurt you, have they?' she asked.

Harry shrugged his shoulders and gazed down at the dirty floor of the shed.

'Why were you hurting yourself?' Once again there was no response. 'Harry, why were you hitting yourself? You have made those bruises. Why?'

'I don't know,' he mumbled.

'Those marks look painful, why don't you let me look at them.' Harry flinched at every step as she moved slowly towards him. 'It's alright I just want to look at the bruises.'

Bronnie lifted his fringe and saw bruises in the hairline, then rolled up his sleeves and saw more marks up the length of his arm.

'Oh, my dear boy!' Harry began to cry uncontrollably. The tears flowed in a cataract of emotion and he burrowed his face into Bronnie's chest, who, in turn, wrapped her arms around him and softly kissed his head. 'It's okay, let's take you home.'

Dai had had a productive morning of writing. No work as yet on the commissioned children's book, but a poem and a short story had sufficed very nicely. At least the words were beginning to reappear, he thought. He waited beneath the Havelock house for Hemi to call by with an anticipation and excitement that the little boy would be proud of. He wanted to see his little friend to tell of his moment of existential realisation, despite the fact that he knew that Hemi would have no idea what he was talking about. He just wanted to tell someone, and as Bronnie was tied up with work, a little Maori child he had known for a matter of weeks seemed just as sensible an option. He also wanted to talk to him about the fiery events of the previous night. He wanted to know where he was and clear up the mystery of the tall man in his room. Most of all he wanted to see his friend. In the short time that Dai had known Hemi he had grown to love his little quirks and eccentricities, his beautifully impertinent manner, as well as his kindness and the simple love he could give with his smile. However, the day came and went without any sign of Hemi. Dai waited for hours for the familiar sound of the patter of little steps at the bottom of the garden but all he heard was the sound of the chaffinches calling from the treetops.

Bronnie led Harry up the scruffy garden path to his house and stood on the porch holding his hand before knocking twice. She could feel Harry's hand trembling in hers, but this time she knew that he shook not in fear of his Mother's hands, but because a secret was about to be exposed. The boy gave a frightened sigh as Mrs Stone finally opened the door.

'What do you want?' she said fiercely.

'I'm sorry,' replied Bronnie earnestly. 'Please, can I come in?'

Mrs Stone thought for a moment. She looked deep into Bronnie's eyes, searching for truth and sincerity. Bronnie suspected that the woman had suffered fools too gladly in the past and so she afforded her time to apply her judgement.

'Okay.'

'Thank you.'

Mrs Stone told Harry to go to his room so that she and Bronnie could talk. Bronnie made her way slowly and respectfully into the darkness of the house. On the sofa a duvet was laid out and there was a pillow at one end. At the side of a sofa there was a plastic bowl from which the smell of bleach drifted. On the coffee table there was a pile of tablets in square and rectangular white boxes, others in their silver foil packets. Bronnie recognised the extended names of the tablets – the painkillers, the sedatives and the anti-depressants. She saw the nutritional milkshakes and the cream for mouth ulcers.

'Excuse the mess,' said Mrs Stone.

'Oh, no it's fine,' replied Bronnie. 'You should see my house and I don't even have children.'

'That hasn't always been the case though has it?'

Bronnie was taken aback by the comment. 'No, it hasn't. How can you tell?'

'People aren't that hard to work out.'

'You think?'

'Yes.' The two sat down on the tatty sofa. 'You are passionate about children.'

'I am, yes,' said Bronnie 'but surely that can be said about most teachers.'

'Not really.' Mrs Stone sat back in her chair and winced as a sharp pain ran through her body. Bronnie squinted her eyes. 'Anyway your passion for children is so…'

'So?' asked Bronnie expectantly.

Mrs Stone struggled to find the right words. 'It has blinded you.'

Bronnie realized what Harry's mother was getting at. She smiled an apology at Mrs Stone.

'You knew that Harry was hurting himself, didn't you.'

'Well of course I did, I might be a shit mother but I'm not an idiot.'

'I never said you were…'

Mrs Stone interrupted, 'You didn't have to. Your manner all but shouted it from the roof-tops.'

'Well, why didn't you tell anyone?' asked Bronnie sheepishly.

'Who could I tell?'

'The school, me...'

'And what would they do then?'

Bronnie searched for the right answer. 'Well they would... we could have...'

'They would have taken him away from me.' She looked deep into Bronnie's eyes. 'He's all I have. I'm all he has.'

'And what about Harry?' This time it was Mrs Stone's turn to look guilty. 'He's sick, he needs help.'

'I've spoken to him so many times. I have told him not to do it.'

'I don't think it's as simple as that.'

Mrs Stone looked mildly insulted. 'I said I wasn't an idiot.'

'No, I know,' said Bronnie, as she looked at the medication once more. 'You're sick too... aren't you?'

Mrs Stone was just about to deny it as Bronnie picked up an empty packet of tablets.

'What is it?' asked Bronnie.

'Cancer.' Bronnie closed her eyes and felt her heart sink as it had when she first learned of Ieuan's diagnosis.

'I'm so sorry.'

'Breast cancer. It is in the early stages.'

'What is the prognosis?'

'Depends,' replied Mrs Stone.

'On what?'

'It depends whether I have a mastectomy or not. The chemo isn't enough. The only way to eradicate it is to have the surgery.'

'You have to.'

'It's that simple is it?'

'It is when you have a son to care for.'

'I just don't have the fight anymore. I am tired of fighting,' said Mrs Stone. 'I am so tired.'

'And what about Harry?' said Bronnie. 'He needs you.'

Mrs Stone got up, walked painfully and gingerly to the fireplace and picked up a picture of Harry.

'He was always a kind little boy. He still is. He takes on so much pain. When his father walked out on us two years ago, even at an early age he believed it was his fault. He thought he had been bad. I kept telling him that it was nobody's fault. But he couldn't get it out of his head. It was around this time that he began to become more and more withdrawn. He used to have friends around but after a while they stopped coming. Then I got sick and…'

Mrs Stone became emotional. Her voice trembled and broke. She took in a deep breath and tried to compose herself.

'Then what?' pressed Bronnie.

'Well, we don't have any family. My husband's family are all in Australia, both my parents are gone I have no brothers or sisters. So it's just us. When I went in for chemo I had no option but to take Harry with me. I used to give him some money for magazines, we would take books and games, you know, things to keep him occupied. I never told him the real reason I was in there. But he knew it was serious.' Mrs Stone ran her ashen fingers over the frame and then caressed Harry's gentle features in the photo. 'Then we would come home and I would be up all night, throwing up. He could hear me crying, in pain, in agony. That's when he started to hurt himself. I started to notice the bruises on his arms. The funny thing is, I thought he got them at school. I thought he got the marks from a fight in the playground. His cheekbone was swollen and he had a black eye. He told me that he fell but I was all ready to come into the school and complain. Then one morning I caught him punching himself in the face while he was in the bath.'

'What did he say about it?'

'Nothing. He still hasn't said anything about it. But I know why he does it.'

'Why?' asked Bronnie.

'It's his way of taking my pain away. It's because he loves me.' The tears began to flow freely from Mrs Stone's eyes. She was right about her fight, there wasn't enough strength to hold back the tears. 'Every time he punches himself, every time he thumps his arm until it bruises, every time he hurts himself he believes it's my pain he's feeling.'

'He needs help.'

'I know,' she sobbed.

'You need help.'

'But there is no one.'

Bronnie rose from her seat and gently took the picture from Mrs Stone's hand and placed it back on the fireplace.

'There is me.'

Mrs Stone looked at Bronnie through weeping eyes and saw the truth and trust within her. She moved forward and fell into Bronnie's arms. Her pain was so acute that she began to pound Bronnie's chest with her head as they embraced. As she allowed his mother to release her pain, fears and sadness all over her, Bronnie saw Harry emerge out of the darkness and stand in the doorway. She smiled at Harry who, for the very first time, smiled back.

12. THE SEARCH

It had been two weeks since Dai had seen Hemi. He had spent a great deal of time outside the Havelock house staring into the bushes at the end of the garden, listening out for the gentle rustle of Hemi's approach, but his little friend was nowhere to be seen. He would stir with excitement when he saw a movement in the trees, but would feel the disappointment run through his veins and into his heart, when he realized that it was little more than a wandering breeze.

Bronnie had been to Harry's house everyday during that point, and had even taken time off work so that she could take Mrs Stone for treatment at the hospital. In that time, the early shoots of friendship had started to blossom between the two. Harry was seen by a child psychologist and was on his own road to recovery.

However, the wound between Dai and Bronnie had not yet healed. Conversations between husband and wife were still trivial and inconsequential. Despite initiating their own separate grieving processes they had yet to come to terms with it as a couple. Ieuan's name was always on the tip of their tongues yet neither would allow the name to drip-drop into a discussion. There was still a lack of intimacy between the two of them. Nights were still cold between them even though the fire of their love had never been, and never could be extinguished. Neither had spoken to the other about their young friends and the secrecy between them both ensured that another wall was erected.

The first heavy rains of the year had arrived. Dai sat beneath the shelter of the house and watched the water pour from the guttering and into huge puddles on the lawn. His thoughts drifted towards Hemi. What had happened to him? Where was he? What had he seen at Hemi's house that night? Finally, Dai resolved to head through the forest, down the mountainside to the little house by the water. He walked slowly and steadily through the rain, holding on to the protruding branches for security. The water soaked through his clothes and soon all he could feel was the coldness of the rain. His mind was racing with thoughts of Hemi and within the din of the precipitation he could hear his little friend's voice, laughing and mocking him.

At last the house came into view. He made his way to Hemi's bedroom window and looked in through the rain cascading down the pane. The room was empty. The toys were gone, as was the bed, the wardrobe, along with any trace of Hemi, or indeed, anyone. He called out to Hemi, but was greeted with only the continuing din of the storm. Confused and concerned, he headed around to the front of the house and saw that the front door was open.

'Hello!' he called. 'Anybody home? Hemi?'

Once again no reply was forthcoming, so Dai pushed the front door open carefully. The door squeaked, creaked and closed behind him with a slam. Dai was startled. He walked though the empty hall to a small living area. There were bright white squares and rectangles on greying walls where pictures had once hung. The carpet had been rolled up and left in an untidy heap at in the corner of the room. A cast iron stove was left open with a tin cup on the top.

Dai went from one empty room to another, before finally stepping into Hemi's bedroom. Once again, the room was stripped, bare and silent, but for the echoing laughter of Hemi in his head.

Heading back out into the rain, he walked toward the waterside and came upon a sodden pile of charcoal and ash. Within the remnants of the fire he saw the pictures and posters which once hung on Hemi's wall. He noticed melted plastic toy soldiers, charred painted pictures and piles of children's clothing which had not completely burned.

Dai had a flutter in his stomach and his concerns for Hemi started to rise into his heart. He was worried for his little friend; where was he? Was he safe? But more disturbing was how the tall dark man fitted into the scheme of things. He stood still on the sooty ground and barely felt the torrents of rain pouring down on him. He couldn't ask Bronnie about one of her own pupils because safeguarding and confidentiality had to be applied. More importantly, he would have to tell her about his friendship with the little boy. He could imagine what she might say and how she might say it. She would, he surmised, feel that bonding with another child was tantamount to betraying the memory of their late son. Yet, as the rain began to fall, the only thing that concerned him was finding his little friend.

The police station at Havelock was little more than an office. A single cell at the end of the room was ornamented with delicate spider webs. It had clearly not been used in a long, long time. Sitting either end of a large desk were two men who could not, it seemed, be more different. The first was a young, skinny, fair-haired officer who seemed gaunt and pale. Dai wagered that he would come out second best with his own baton, much less a hardened criminal. The second was a corpulent sexagenarian whose gut spilled over his waistline and all but covered his accessories belt. Dai stood before the two and waited for them to greet him. Neither was in a hurry to do so and Dai had to cough to fully attract their attention. The slim Constable Mitchell finally graced Dai with his attention.

'Yeah?' he said without even meeting Dai's eyes.

Dai ignored the rudeness. 'I think...' he hesitated, 'I think I need to report a missing child.'

'You think?' replied the smarmy junior ranker.

'Well, I don't know if he is missing.'

'Look, either he is or he isn't.'

'It's not as simple as that.'

'Why not?'

'Look, I don't have time for this crap!' said Dai losing his patience. 'I am trying to tell you that there is a child and I think he might be in danger.'

'In danger of what?'

'I DON'T FUCKING KNOW!' shouted Dai.

At that point, Sergeant Moore pulled his obese body out from behind the desk and joined in the discussion.

'How long has he been missing?' he wheezed.

'I don't know.'

'You don't know?'

'No...' he sighed, 'a couple of weeks maybe.'

'A couple of weeks!' said Moore incredulously. 'And you're only coming to us with this now?'

'Look, he's not my child...' replied Dai.

'Well whose kid is it?'

'I don't know!'

'Well who are his parents?'

'I don't know,' replied Dai, 'but his name is Hemi. He's a Maori boy.'

'Bloody hell mate, you ain't giving us much to go on are you?'

'Well I...'

'You come in here and tell us a child you don't know has gone missing,' said Moore. 'You don't know how long he's been gone, you don't know who he belongs to...'

'I do know who he is, ' interrupted Dai. 'His name is Hemi. He lives by the water.'

'Everybody in this town lives by the bloody water,' interjected the smarmy Mitchell.

'Look,' Dai put his hands out and tried to calm the situation, 'you must have some kind of file, some kind of search you can do on the computer.'

'I don't need a computer. I know everyone in this town... except you.'

'Well, then you will know this boy.'

Moore ambled over to the coffee machine and poured a drink. He returned to his chair and put his feet on the desk.

'What did you say his name was?'

'Hemi,' answered Dai.

'Hemi... what?'

'I only know his first name.' Moore rolled his eyes. 'Look, a minute ago you were telling me that you knew everyone in this town, so do you know this child or not?'

Moore took a long sip of his coffee. 'Nope!'

'So you are going to do nothing?'

'Well what do you want us to do, for Christ's sake?'

'I want you to find this child.' The pair looked at each other and shook their heads before mumbling something derogatory which Dai couldn't hear properly. Dai began to head out of the station but turned back again as his memory was stirred. 'Wait a minute.'

'Oh, what now?' whined Mitchell.

'There was a man in his house.'

'In whose house?' asked Moore.

'Hemi's!'

'Right and what did this man look like?'

'It was dark,' said Dai 'I couldn't see properly he was a big man. Tall.'

'And?' enquired Moore.

'Well, maybe he's got something to do with Hemi's disappearance.'

'Look, mate, when you've got a bit more for us to go on, let us know. But bloody hell, I can't initiate an investigation on that kind of information.'

Dai was in disbelief. 'So that's it, is it?'

'That's it,' said Moore.

'Well thanks,' Dai stormed out of the station. 'Thanks for nothing.'

That evening, writing was the last thing on Dai's mind. Nothing was able to remove thoughts of Hemi from his head. His fears kept whirling around, becoming more and more intense. Talk at the dinner table that night was quieter and more stilted than usual. Dai, when questioned by Bronnie about his day, was distant and subdued. He left his dinner almost untouched and got up from his chair.

'I'm not hungry,' he said. 'I'm going out for a walk.'

Once again, in the fading light, Dai headed off through the forest where the ferns fanned out before him and the dusk chorus called, cried, whistled and chattered. The clouds above denied Havelock the luxury of moonlight, so Dai almost felt his way through the trees until he came upon Hemi's house. As he drew close to the house he saw the light of a small bonfire near the water's edge. The faint smell of smoke wafted through the air and rose into the night sky. Dai crept closer and closer to the house, inching delicately, quietly and nervously toward the fire, tiptoe by tiptoe. As before, Dai's heart pounded, he could hear his own heavy breathing and he felt flutters in the pit of his stomach. As he stumbled his way to the side of the house he saw the tall, dark figure arrive again. He came from the boat, once again with a petrol canister and a bin liner of something. Dai watched incredulously as the tall, bulky man emptied the contents of the black bag on to the fire.

Dai crouched down and then laid on his front. Slowly, hand by hand, leg by leg, he crawled closer to the fire to identify the man. He needed some positive evidence for the police to take his concerns seriously. As the indeterminate light of the fire flickered across the man's body, it illuminated certain features. The revelation was slow and Dai's eyes struggled in the darkness. First came the sight of flip-flops crushed beneath the weight of enormous feet. Another flicker of light – traditional Maori tattoos on the arms and body, which was lightly clad by a weightlifting vest. Finally, as the flames grew higher, he saw the face at last. It was the face which had terrified him before, first in the supermarket and then in the school yard. It was Ruru.

Dai recoiled as Ruru continued to fuel the fire with strange odds and ends, which he assumed belonged to Hemi. His concerns for his little friend intensified. Where was Hemi? He entertained a number of dark and gruesome thoughts about what Ruru might have done to the little boy and began to frighten himself. He felt uncomfortable twinges in his stomach, pins and needles in the tips of his fingers and toes, and once more he struggled to regulate his heartbeat and breathing. Slowly and carefully he crept backwards until he was back in the forest, from where he made his way back home.

Playing Beneath the Havelock House

That night, Dai refused to even fight his insomnia. While Bronnie slept peacefully in bed, he paced up and down the house, sat out on the veranda watching and feeding the possums, made tea and then more tea. He kept hearing Hemi's mischievous giggle and remembered some of the funny things he said. What he wouldn't give to hear the boy call him Pākehā once more.

By the time Bronnie rose and made her way into the kitchen everything was ready - the cereal, the orange juice, the toast and the tea.

'Have you been up all night?' she asked taking her seat at the table.

'Yeah,' he rubbed his reddening eyes, 'I just couldn't settle. You got a busy day today?'

'Yep, as ever.'

Dai thought for a moment about how he could manipulate the conversation to find out more about Ruru.

'So…' He paused. 'How are you getting on with everyone at the school?'

'Okay. Why do you ask?'

'No reason,' he said, 'just making conversation.'

'Well, Mrs Anders is still as pompous as ever and she evidently thinks of me as a loose cannon. Mrs Havers is a timid little thing, but lovely. Mrs Simpson is wonderful, very old-school, but sweet. George is George and he would do anything for anyone, although,' she added, 'he doesn't have much time for Ruru.'

'Oh, he's the big Maori guy, isn't he?'

'Yes,' she shivered. 'He gives me the creeps.'

'Why?' asked Dai.

'I don't know. It's the way he looks, you know all those tattoos, his size and he hardly ever speaks. I'm always wondering what he's thinking. He's a criminal too, you know.'

'No, I didn't know.' Dai's heart sank down another level. 'What did he do?'

'I don't know exactly. I don't think anyone does really. He's been at the school for a while as part of his release conditions. Something like a community service, I think.'

'You mean he was in jail?'

'Yeah,' Bronnie crunched into a piece of toast.

'I see,' said Dai. 'What's his surname?'

'Ngata,' she replied. 'Why d'you ask?'

'Oh, no reason,' he took a sip of orange juice, 'just curious.'

'Well,' said Bronnie, forcing down the last crusts of toast, 'I'd better get going.'

They kissed coldly on the lips and parted.

So as not to arouse suspicion, Dai waited until he heard the sound of Bronnie's tyres pulling away from the gravel drive. Then, like a man possessed, he put on his shoes and began running into Havelock. His legs and arms were laden with the weight of fatigue. As weariness and breathlessness set in, his strides shortened until he was reduced to a walk. In the warmth of the morning sun and in the breezeless sky, he felt the sweat dripping down the side of his face and down the nape of his neck, before trickling down the rungs of his spine. Visions of Hemi's face spurred him on, while unwelcome thought of what might have happened to his little friend pushed him even further.

Out of breath, with his pulse racing and his head throbbing, Dai finally made it to the Police station. Bursting through the doors he rang the bell on the counter continuously until the portly Moore eventually dragged himself up from his early morning coffee, leaving Mitchell reading the newspaper.

'What d'you want now?'

'I want you to find Hemi!' demanded Dai.

'Oh yes, of course, Hemi,' replied Moore facetiously. 'The child you don't know, who has been taken by someone else you don't know to some where you don't know.'

'Listen to me you arsehole…'

'…I beg your pardon.'

'Look! A child is missing, I do not wish to stand here arguing with you. There was a man at the boy's house setting fire to toys and clothing.'

'What man?'

'His name is Ruru Ngata.'

'Ruru?' said Moore familiarly.

'Ngata!' Dai wiped the sweat from his brow. 'You know about him don't you?'

'What do you mean?'

'You know exactly what I mean? He's just out of jail.'

'Oh. I see, Mr Sherlock-bloody-Holmes' said Mitchell, 'and you think that makes him a kidnapper, do you?'

'Well, surely it's worth at least checking out, rather than sitting here with your thumb up your arse.'

'Now listen to me, you bloody pom. I'm not going to go charging into a situation here.' Moore tried to stand tall. He pushed his shoulders back and allowed his belly to cast a slightly shallower shadow over his feet. 'I'm not going to go up to a man and ask him if he has taken a child, just like that.'

'Jesus!' exclaimed Dai.

'And anyway what were you doing on Ruru's property?'

'Looking for Hemi!'

'You sure you weren't trespassing?'

'You are kidding right?' said an exasperated Dai.

'I could just as easily charge you!'

'Fucking hell!' Dai paused for a while and tried to regain his composure. 'You are not going to do a thing, are you?'

Moore did not say a word. He did not have to. Dai knew full well that, due to his lack of evidence and the incompetence of Moore and his deputy, he would have to solve the mystery of Hemi's disappearance by himself. He was on his own.

13 WAITING ROOMS AND REVELATIONS

During the half-hour drive south to the quaint town of Blenheim, Bronnie and Mrs Stone talked politely and, as new friends do, began to share little pieces of their previous history. Mrs Stone had been married to a captain of the Interlink ferry, which traversed the Cook Strait daily. It was a good job and they enjoyed affluence and happiness until a waitress from Wellington sullied the relationship not long after Harry's birth. Her husband left and had been absent ever since, with not so much as a birthday card or a Christmas present for Harry. In return Bronnie told her of the difficulties that she and Dai had faced since Ieuan's death. Adversaries for weeks, the two were now each other's only friend and companion. As they continued south from Havelock another question was on Bronnie's mind.

'You know, through all of this, one thing is still perplexing me?'

Mrs Stone looked at her, concerned that the next question might open up old wounds or threaten the buds of the friendship.

'What's your name?'

Mrs Stone laughed softly at first, and then with more vigour as she let go of her coldness and pretense. Her laugh was infectious and soon Bronnie began to laugh uncontrollably. Eventually the hilarity subsided. For some unknown reason, Bronnie had continued to refer to her new companion by her surname, to the point that it had become almost a nickname. Likewise, Bronnie was Mrs Ifans to Harry's mother.

'Well?' insisted Bronnie.

'Bobby,' she said. 'Well, my real name is Roberta! But everyone calls me Bobby.'

'Well, Bobby,' smiled Bronnie, 'I'm pleased to make your acquaintance.'

Soon they had parked up at Blenheim Hospital and a gentle if slightly awkward silence ensued. On their previous visit to the hospital, Bronnie had waited in the car while Mrs Stone had a pre-op appointment. This day would be different.

'Would you mind coming in with me?' asked Bobby.

Bronnie could see from the look in her eyes that this was less of a request and more of a plea. Bronnie reached out her hand and gripped Bobby firmly.

'Of course!'

Following the long winding walk down white, sterile corridors, they found their way to Wellington Ward. A young and attractive nurse, complete with a smile and simple kindness, guided Bobby to her hospital bed right by the window and then began to paste on monitor pads, insert needles, draw blood and start the infusion of chemicals. Throughout the ordeal Bronnie held Bobby's hands. She noticed in her new friend the same pale hands, colourless fingernails and, occasionally, the same frightened smile she saw in Ieuan and she could feel her heart break a little. Yet, she remained steadfast and strong for Bobby.

The hours passed quickly. Bobby and Bronnie spent their time filling in the story of their lives. The significant events, deaths, marriages, births, career moves and such like had been covered in the first weeks of their burgeoning friendship, now it was time to colour the relationship with as many nuances as time would allow. They talked about hobbies, favourite films and music, pet hates and character traits. In the few moments of comfortable silence that only friends seem to experience, Bobby would look out of the window and watch the sun play hide and seek in the scattering clouds.

Finally, as the treatment drew to a close and the syringes, wires and monitor pads were removed, Bobby dragged herself up the bed and sat upright.

'If I don't make it through this…'

'Don't start that,' said Bronnie, 'you're going to be…'

'…Don't say 'fine,' please.'

'But it's true.'

Bobby paused for a while. 'When I was pregnant with Harry, I knew it. I knew it instantly. I didn't even need the test. When my husband was screwing someone else, I knew. I didn't even have to look in his eyes. I just knew it. I could feel it. And when I had cancer… I just knew something was wrong. Call it a woman's intuition. I can feel it now.'

'What are you saying?'

'Harry.'

'What about him?' asked Bronnie, although she knew exactly where the conversation was heading.

'He has no one other than me.' She ran her fingers though her straggly, thinning hair. 'His father is gone, we've no family… they'll put him in a home.'

'I'm sure it won't come to that,' said Bronnie as convincingly as she could.

'Will you take care of Harry?'

Bronnie was struck by Bobby's directness. The question was like an arrow which pierced her heart, her mind and her conscience at the same time. Within a second her mind played out a number of scenarios. She saw her flat refusal and then saw Harry languishing in a corner of a children's home. She imagined Dai's reaction, his anger and his sorrow, the ensuing arguments, the shouting matches and the long silences. Finally, she saw Ieuan. What would he have wanted? She wondered. Would it dishonour his memory to allow another child into their lives? And, not least, Harry's similarity to Ieuan would, she felt, be a constant reminder of what she had lost.

'Do you know what you are asking me?'

'Of course I do.'

'I don't know what to say.'

'Say, yes.'

Bronnie shifted uneasily in the chair at the side of the bed. 'But you hardly know me.'

'I know enough.'

'What do you mean?'

'You looked out for Harry when you thought he was being hurt, you're here with me now.'

'Yes but…'

Bobby interjected, 'And I know you need to love someone again, I can see that in your eyes.'

Bronnie paused for a moment. 'What can you see?'

'You're frightened. More frightened than me.'

'What are you talking about?' asked Bronnie.

Bobby sighed and spent a moment assembling the right words in her head.

'You loved your son.'

'Of course.'

'You loved him with everything you had. Now you grieve with everything you have.' Bronnie was silent, struck dumb by the truth in Bobby's words. 'You're frightened to love again, in case you feel a pain like this again. It's like you think that love is a poison which might taste sweet, but soon turns sour and deadly. But it isn't.' Bobby smiled. 'Love is the cure.'

Bronnie sighed softly. 'It seems you know me more than I gave you credit for.'

'Then say yes.'

'I can't just say yes, you are asking me to take care of child. This is flesh and blood. I can't just agree to something like that on a whim.'

Bronnie moved slowly toward the window and looked out over the hospital grounds which were bathed in sunshine.

'It's not as simple as that,' she said.

'It's as simple as you want it to be.'

'No, it isn't,' Bronnie ran her hands through her hair and turned once again to face Bobby. 'There are the legalities of the whole thing, for one.'

'I'll take care of that.'

'How?'

'I'll take care of it!' insisted Bobby. 'I'll make you a godparent, Harry was never christened. That will add weight.'

'I don't know,' sighed Bronnie. 'It all seems so…'

'What?' asked Bobby.

'I mean, how can you be so…?'

'Yes?'

'How can you be so matter-of-fact about the whole thing?'

'Because that fact of the matter is that in the near future I could be little more than a feast for worms.'

'You don't know that.'

'I know my body.' Bobby reached for a glass of water at the side of her bed and allowed the sun outside to illuminate her face softly. 'I can feel it.'

'So what then?' said Bronnie, shrugging her shoulders. 'You are just going to give up?'

'Please! Don't!'

'Are you really going to give in to this? Give up on Harry?'

'It's not a case of giving up, it's…'

'What?' demanded Bronnie.

'You have to be realistic about these things.' Bronnie watched as the glimmer of a tear began to well up in Bobby's eye. 'As long as I can I will fight this. I will fight it with every fibre, every muscle, every sinew, every breath and every heartbeat. But I am only fighting for time. I am fighting for another Christmas, maybe another birthday. I want to spend as much of the time I have left watching Harry grow. Now all of this is out in the open I can...' She paused just as the tear weaved a wandering line down the undulations of her face. 'Oh, I don't know. I suppose I'm no different to anyone else. We're all fighting for time really.'

Bronnie reached out her hand and held Bobby's tightly. She smiled. She wanted to reassure her friend but was wary of committing.

'I'll see you right,' she said.

The Mussel Pot Café was deserted when Dai arrived that morning. He ordered a coffee and set up his laptop. While he waited for it to hum into action, he looked out of the window and watched the cars running intermittently through the quietness of the town. A greying man disturbed his stare as he placed the steaming coffee in front of him with a kind smile.

Dai hooked up to the internet and searched first through the archives of the New Zealand Herald and then the local Marlborough Express. He typed in Ruru's name next to a little magnifying glass icon and waited as the results were loaded. A link emerged with the tag line 'Marae Destroyed by Fire.' Dai clicked on the link and saw a picture of a charred piece of wood carving in a pile of smouldering ashes. He read on.

The fire at the marae three miles south of Havelock destroyed all of the buildings and left little but ash in its wake. Local residents reported seeing the flames climbing high into the darkness at around midnight. The fire, which could be seen from the hills around Havelock, was started deliberately according to Fire Chief Tom Anderson. At the height of the fire, forces from Picton and Seddon had joined the Havelock firefighters. There were no reports of injuries or fatalities. A twenty-five year-old man, Ruru Ngata was arrested shortly afterwards on suspicion of arson and taken into police custody.

Dai continued to read on. He read through the details of Ruru's arrest, subsequent trial and conviction. The severity of the prison term, eleven years was due to Ruru maintaining a silence as to the reasons for his actions and refusing to offer an apology to the elders of the marae and those who had lost their property and possessions. The damage was estimated to be in the hundreds of thousands of dollars.

Dai wondered why Ruru would have done such an act? The Maori, renowned as a strong and close-knit community, were intrinsically linked - socially, historically, politically and culturally - by the marae. To cause such devastation was to undermine everything that Ruru would have stood for. The burning of the marae would have been a great insult to not only the community, but also Ruru's ancestors.

The compulsion to investigate for himself was too much for Dai to contain. He closed his laptop down, slurped the last dregs of his coffee, leaving the congealed sugar remains at the bottom of the mug and headed out on to the main road. As Bronnie had taken the car, Dai had no option but the follow the roadside the three miles south to the marae on foot. The long walk gave him time to run through various scenarios in his head. He entertained the possible and the ludicrous as the cars sped by. The imagination that he relied so heavily upon for his livelihood now tested him to his limits. His creativity, until now, had been charged with creating gentle images – unicorns, fantastic lands, far-off worlds - for the minds of children. Yet the pictures in his head now were of a very different nature – bloody and brutal.

By the time that he arrived at the marae, gentle rains had started to fall. As per the custom, Dai waited at the gate to the marae until he saw an old man walking the grounds. Dai casually cleared his throat to attract the man's attention. Aided by a walking stick, the elderly man made his way unsteadily to the gate.

'Yes?'

'Hello,' said Dai nervously, 'Um... I'm... I'm an author.'

'An author?' said the man suspiciously.

'Yes.'

'I see.' The man looked Dai up and down.

'I'm... I'm writing a book about... Maori history in Marlborough.'

'You're not a tourist then?' he asked in a gravely voice.

'No, I live in Havelock. My wife teaches at the school.'

'That's alright then, I haven't got time to go through all that. So what do you want Mr Author?'

'Well I heard that this marae was destroyed some time ago.'

'Well it looks like you've done your research Mr Author.'

'Dai.'

'What?' replied the man incredulously.

'No, it's okay. That's my name.'

'Okay, Dai.' The man relented, my name is Kahu.'

There was an awkward pause as Kahu offered an expectant look.'

'Well?' asked a perplexed Dai.

'Well are we going to greet properly or what?'

'Oh, I'm sorry,' said Dai. He offered his hand over the gate to the marae and was firmly pulled into a hongi. As their noses and forehead met in the traditional manner, Dai could smell the tobacco on Kahu's breath.

'So what do you want to know?'

'Well, can you tell me what happened that night?' asked Dai.

'You'd better come in then.'

'Is that okay?'

The man smiled, 'Well it's not the usual protocol. I should send my boy to you and issue a te wero.'

'Sorry?'

'It's the challenge laid out to a stranger who comes on to the marae. To see if you are a friend or an enemy. My boy comes out to you with the spear and puts a fern on the floor before you. You pick it up, you are a friend. You leave it, you are an enemy.' He looked at Dai once more and smiled. 'But, looking at you, you don't look strong enough to be an enemy, you skinny bastard.'

Dai laughed, 'Oh, thanks very much, I think.'

'No, I think I could probably kick your arse.'

Kahu opened the gates and Dai made his way on to the marae. A straight tarmac path cut through two lawns which were perfectly manicured, luscious and green. At the end of the path was an ornate building, complete with traditional Maori carvings in red wood.

'This is the wharenui,' said Kahu. 'It's the meeting place. This has been totally rebuilt. There was nothing left after the fire. The whole place was in ruins.'

'Was anybody hurt?'

'My boy, Tama, along with some of the others from our iwi who fought the fire until the fire brigade came, they suffered. Smoke inhalation mostly. We just had buckets and garden hoses, we didn't stand a bloody chance. Thankfully, nobody was seriously hurt though.'

'Was it arson?' asked Dai.

'You've heard that?'

'Is it true?'

Kahu stopped in his stride. 'I'm afraid so.'

'One of your own?' asked Dai

'Ruru Ngata.'

'What happened?'

'Let's go and sit down.' said Kahu. 'You like tea?'

It was only a few yards up another straight path to the wharekai. A small dining area with circular tables laid out ready for a gathering later that evening. As Kahu made the tea, Dai sat alone in the area and looked at photographs on the wall of the previous wharenui in its former glory, alongside a picture of its destruction.

'Here you are,' said Kahu. 'Get this down you.'

Dai slurped his tea and offered his gratitude.

'So, what happened then?'

'It was a late summer evening,' replied Kahu. 'We had just finished a wedding party. Most of the guests had gone and I was locking up when I began to smell the smoke. I saw the smoke billowing out of the door of the wharenui. So I ran to it – back when I could run – and opened the door. The heat was incredible. I looked inside and already the flames were reaching to the ceiling. The heke soon came crashing down.'

'Heke?'

'The rafters,' said Kahu, 'they are the ribs of the wharenui.'

'I see.'

'There was nothing we could do.' Kahu took a large gulp of his tea then wiped his lips on his sleeve. 'The fire was too intense.'

'What about Ruru?' asked Dai.

'He was always a bit quiet, but he was okay. Great rugby player. He said hello and helped out from time to time among the iwi. But he split from his wife, I forget her name now, and he became more and more isolated and rarely set foot on the marae. He became volatile, unpredictable and he got into lots of trouble with the police. Nothing much, just stupid brawls and fights in bars. Then one day he was questioned about a missing child who was later found dead not far from here. They took him in for questioning, but there wasn't enough evidence. No witnesses, nothing that would stand up in court. But we knew. I knew.'

'Knew what?'

'That he was responsible for that boy's death.'

'How do you know?'

'Because he told me so.'

'He came to me the night before the fire and asked to speak to me as chief, to confess. He said he wanted help.'

'What did you say?'

'I didn't hang around to hear. I didn't want the responsibility. I thought the less I knew, the better. I told him he would have to go to the police. I said he had to hand himself in.'

'What did he say?' asked Dai.

'Well, let's just say he didn't take it well. And within a few hours the marae was destroyed. He is a dangerous man.' He stood up, swallowed the last dregs of his tea and offered his hand to Dai. 'Now, I'm afraid you'll have to excuse me. I have some duties I have to attend to.'

The aging Kahu left the room unsteadily, leaving Dai alone with his tea and his thoughts.

14. CONFRONTATIONS

The storm was raging like a vengeful god. The sky was as dark as night, although the afternoon was barely over. Dai sat beneath the Havelock house and watched the raindrops bouncing off the patio and saw the lawn begin to flood steadily. Kahu's revelations were trapped in his head and the thought that Hemi was in serious danger worried Dai greatly.

Ruru was a huge man. His physique was enough to send Dai into a cold sweat, but his mystery, his history, his scowl, his silence and his aura were all equally terrifying. Yet Dai knew that in order to find out what had happened to Hemi, he would have to confront him. He would have no help from the incompetent local constabulary. He was on his own and had to act now.

He stepped out from the cover of the protruding house into the deluge of torrential precipitation and began walking down the slippery hillside to Hemi's house. With each step a butterfly would flutter inside his stomach and with every slip on the wet and uneven ground his heart would sink to a new level.

When the fear threatened to overwhelm Dai, he remembered Ieuan. He had been so helpless in the last months of his son's life. All he could do was to make life more comfortable for him. He could dab his brow with a cold wet cloth, he could buy him a magazine from the hospital shop, he could read one of his own stories, he could hold his hand, kiss him, hug him; but he couldn't save him. Now it was within his control to find out exactly what happened to Hemi and, if it wasn't too late, perhaps save him from Ruru.

As the rain hammered down, it seemed that nature had decided to hide from the storm. The calling of the tuis, the blackbirds and all the other wildlife had been muted to an eerie silence. All that Dai could hear as he made his way through the forest was the sound of his feet squelching in the mud, the cacophonic din of the rain drum-rolling on the leaves and the incessant pounding of his own pulse.

Finally, the clearing by Hemi's house came into view. Dai made his way to Hemi's bedroom window, wiped as much of the cascading rain off the pane and peered in through the glass. There was no sign of Hemi.

With a little muscle the flaking window frame stuttered and staggered open. Dai pushed the window up as far as it could go, then climbed in. The room was cold. He closed the window behind him and ran his fingers through his hair to rinse away the rain before sitting on the floor. He sat motionless. He blinked hard. His eyes looked down at the floor. He saw the comics scattered over the carpet, the matchbox cars which were sprinkled ad hoc in one corner or the room and a deflated rugby ball in the other. He closed his eyes and imagined that, for just one second, everything was as it was before Hemi's disappearance. Perhaps he would walk through the door with his cheeky smile, perhaps it wasn't raining at all; perhaps, perhaps, perhaps. He blinked once again and as before, the room was empty.

Then, just as his mind was beginning to drift into a dream, the bedroom door opened. Dai leapt to his feet like a lightning bolt. There in the doorway was the fearsome figure of Ruru.

'What the fuck are you doing in here?'

Dai said nothing. His reply was trapped behind his fear. He simply starred at Ruru.

'Are you deaf?' asked Ruru, taking a step closer to the quivering Dai. 'What are you doing here?'

Then, as an image of Hemi raced through his mind, a calmness descended over Dai. It was the calmness of a man who had accepted his own fate. His head was almost preparing him for an act of violence, while his heart needed to know what had happened to his little friend.

'I could ask you the same thing.'

'What did you say?' said Ruru, tensing and flexing his muscles.

Dai swallowed. 'You heard me.'

'Who the fuck do you think you are?'

'I'm Dai.'

'Well, Dai, I'm not going to tell you again. You get back out through that window' he took a step closer, 'or I'll throw you through it.'

Dai took in a deep breath and closed his eyes.

'Where is he?' demanded Dai.

'Where's who?' asked an irate Ruru.

Despite all his fear he stepped forward, one step closer to Ruru.

'Don't play games with me.' Dai stood as firm as his nerves would allow. 'Where is he?'

Ruru stepped forward once more and grabbed Dai by the throat. He thrust him against the bedroom wall and began to lift him until Dai was on tip-toes. Then he moved nose to nose with Dai, who could smell stale alcohol on the giant's breath.

'I could kill you!' he snarled, and snapped his fingers. 'Like that.'

'No you couldn't,' whispered Dai though Ruru's vice-like grip, 'I'm already dead.'

'What are you talking about?'

'I'm not saying anything else until you tell me where he is?'

Ruru squeezed a little tighter. 'Who?'

'Hemi!'

Ruru's eyes widened and Dai could see a storm raging behind them. With one more squeeze of his enormous hand Ruru, lifted Dai off the ground and threw him through the window. Dai felt the decaying window frame crumble upon impact and he winced as he felt shards of glass pierce through the skin on his back. He landed in the flooded mud beneath the window. Ruru lifted the window open fully, so hard that the remaining daggers of glass, which clung precariously to the pane, dropped to the ground. He climbed through the opening, into the storm and once again grabbed Dai.

'What do you know about Hemi?' screamed Ruru.

'You tell me.' Dai was becoming immune to his fear. He felt the trickle of warm blood run from a laceration above his eye and mix with the cold rain running down his face. 'Did you kill him too? Did you kill Hemi?'

'You bastard.' Ruru lifted Dai out of the mud and delivered a punch to his face. Dai felt and heard a crack and new instantly that his cheekbone was broken. The pain surged through his head and neck.

'I didn't kill anyone!' shouted Ruru through the din of the rain.

'Bullshit! I know everything,' screamed Dai. 'I know about the fire, I know about the child you killed. I went to the marae. I saw what you did. They told me you were responsible for a boy's death.'

Ruru stopped. 'You don't know anything!'

'What do you mean?'

Ruru stared straight into Dai's blood soaked eyes, picked him up by the back of his t-shirt and began to drag him through the mud. He pulled him along the sodden lawns of the house, past the charcoaled markings from previous incinerations and out to the decaying boat launch.

'You wanna see Hemi?' he shouted. 'You wanna see the boy? Do you?'

Ruru forced Dai to his knees and then on to his stomach. Then with all his fury he pushed Dai's face into the water. Dai held his breath for as long as he could before Ruru pulled him out of the water to repeat his questions, only to lower his face beneath the wave again. Ruru ducked Dai over and over and each time Dai would inhale as deeply as possible, believing that it would be his last breath. On the final submergence, Dai opened his eyes and saw Hemi lying in the mud beneath the water. Dai was assailed by confusion; was it Hemi or merely a hallucination brought on by the anguish of his physical and mental pain. This time, the trauma precipitated an involuntary inhalation and Dai took in a lung full of water, at which point Ruru pulled him once more from the waves and left him alone to cough up the salty fluid. Then as quickly as the anger had risen in Ruru it retreated and left in its wake a broken man. Dai tried to regulate his breathing, with the blood seeping from the cuts about his body and the pain in his cheekbone pounding in syncopation to his racing heart. Ruru stepped back slowly and sat down against a raised log from the boat launch. He pulled his knees up to his chest and wrapped his bulky arms around his shins.

'He was my boy.'

Dai's heart sank, 'What?'

'He was my son.' His voice softened and suddenly the tyrannical beast was little more than a helpless child. 'Hemi was my son.'

The information was too profound for Dai, 'I don't understand.'

'Neither do I,' replied Ruru.

'What happened?'

Ruru sighed weakly, rubbed the rain off his head and spoke.

'We were all we had. All I had was him, all he had was me. We didn't have much time for the iwi. We were never welcome at the marae. My wife left when Hemi was young. I brought him up on my own. The iwi... I felt abandoned. I tried to be polite but the marae was never a home for me, or Hemi. I wanted him to learn about his ancestors, I wanted him to learn about his history, about our culture. So I taught him all I could. Sometimes we'd visit the marae, but it was always awkward.'

Dai ran his fingers over his inflamed cheekbone, winced, but listened intently.

'I told him stories about the Maori gods, about…'

Dai interrupted, 'Hinenuitepo.'

'How do you know about that?' asked Ruru.

Dai sighed, 'I'll tell you later. Go on.'

'All Hemi ever wanted to do was to please me, to have my approval. I don't think he really knew that he had my approval from the day I first held him.' Ruru allowed the faintest of smiles to grace his face. 'I inherited this place from my father. He used to fish here and collect mussels. I wanted him to learn how to catch a fish. I remember how big and strong I felt when I caught my first fish with my father. I felt like all of my ancestors were in the boat with me. I felt like a leader. I tried to get Hemi to learn to swim. I tried to teach him, but he was terrified of the water. He was ok with me in the boat, but he was petrified of falling in the water. He'd always sit in the middle of the boat, he felt safer there. One night, I got angry with him. I was stupid. I told him that he had to be a man. I said he was weak, that "the weak are never really alive" – that was my father speaking. I didn't mean it. There are lots of things I never meant to do or say.'

'You're not alone there,' said Dai.

'The next morning I woke up and called Hemi to the table for breakfast. He didn't come. Then I saw a note on the fridge door. He said he'd gone to catch a big fish. I came out here and saw that my rowing boat was gone. I looked out across the water and then I saw, way out in the distance, Hemi standing in the boat with a fishing rod. He was flailing it around all over the place. I called out to him. I screamed at him to stay there, that I would come and get him.'

Ruru paused as he relived the moment in real time in his mind.

'Go on,' prompted Dai.

'He must have heard me because he turned around quickly. He must have lost his balance or something, because he tripped and fell overboard. One minute he was there, the next there was a tiny splash and he was gone. I dived in and started swimming but he must have been 500 yards away. I swam as fast as I could. I didn't even think to take my clothes off. I wish I had 'cause they slowed me down. Maybe I could have got to him quicker. When I got to the boat, I couldn't see him anywhere. I kept diving beneath the water around the boat, trying to see him. Finally, I saw him drifting down. He wasn't moving. I swam deeper, reached down, grabbed his wrist and pulled him up. I dragged him into the boat. His body was limp. He was like a rag doll. I tried CPR. I begged. I pleaded to God, I pleaded to my ancestors to save him. I pleaded. "Don't take him! Please don't take my boy." But they took him. They stole my boy from me. They left me there in that little boat with just his body to hold on to. That's all I could do; hold on to him. So I did. I held him and I felt myself die too. As I held him, I looked in the boat and I saw a fish flipping and flapping. My boy had caught a fish. I was so sad, but so proud. My boy caught a fish. He caught a fish.'

With those words, the tears began to flow from Ruru's face and soon Dai began to feel his own sadness rising through his heart as he realised that Hemi was dead. He always had been.

'I picked up the fish and put it back in the water. I imagined Hemi's little soul in that fish, swimming away. I don't know why.'

'I'm sorry,' said Dai.

Ruru tried to regain his composure. 'So that's it. I was responsible for my son's death. He got into that boat for me. He rowed out across these waters to make me proud of him. If I hadn't screamed at him, I wouldn't have frightened him, he wouldn't have taken my boat, he wouldn't have slipped and fallen... he would be alive now. We'd have eaten that fish.'

'It's not your fault,' said Dai softly.

'It's not for me to say that I'm innocent,' said Ruru. 'I was responsible.'

'But nobody could possibly have forseen something like that.'

Ruru continued. 'The iwi offered what they could. They helped pay for some of the expenses after Hemi died. But I had this... rage. Pure rage. It grew inside me. It started to eat me. Day by day it would eat a bit more until I was hollow. I wondered where my ancestors were, where were the gods? I hadn't told anyone why Hemi had taken the boat. I thought that maybe if I confessed to being responsible for his death I might be able to... move on.'

'Who did you talk to?'

'I went to the marae and spoke to Kahu. I told him I needed to say something important, that I had something to confess. I told him I was responsible for a boy's death. I didn't have time to tell him it was Hemi. He wouldn't listen. He wouldn't let me speak, he told me he didn't want to hear anything which would bring shame and misfortune on the marae. He told me to go to the police. I just wanted someone to listen to me.'

'So you set fire to the marae?'

'I thought, I'll bring you misfortune. I'll bring you misfortune that you'd never imagine in your worst nightmares. I hated the iwi, I hated the gods, I hated my ancestors. I hated them for not existing. The only way I could hurt them was to destroy the marae. To destroy everything it stood for. I had nothing else to lose. They arrested me and sent me to jail.'

'And the gods and ancestors...' Dai trod carefully, 'you say they don't exist.'

'How can they? What god or ancestor would do such a thing?'

'What if... what if something exists?'

'Like what?' asked Ruru.

'I don't know.' Dai stood up and walked slowly toward Ruru and then sat down before him. 'I'm not sure if I know anything anymore.'

'I don't understand.'

'How did I know about Hinenuitepo?' asked Dai carefully. 'How did I know that you told him that story?'

'Every Maori child knows that story.'

Dai moved in carefully. 'How do I know you were a rugby player?'

'Around here, there aren't many Maori men over twelve stone who weren't rugby players at some point or other. What are you getting at?'

One step closer. 'How would I know that you sang him Hine e Hine when he woke up after a nightmare on Halloween? He dreamed of a skeleton chasing him.'

This time Ruru looked at Dai differently. He looked deep into his eyes, as if looking for Hemi.

'How do you know about that?' asked Ruru.

Dai paused. He took in a deep breath as the rain continued to dilute the blood still seeping from the wounds around his head and face. He surmised that all he could do now was to simply tell Ruru the truth - or at least the truth as he saw it.

'I've seen Hemi.'

'That's impossible.'

'I know,' said Dai. 'But it's true.'

'It can't be.'

'I've spoken to him. I would speak to him everyday.'

'How would I know these things?' asked Dai.

Ruru looked perplexed, while Dai recalled some of his other meetings with Hemi.

'How would I know that you used to go on holiday to Kaikoura? Your uncle runs a whale-watching business there. How would I know that you tried to teach Hemi how to play the Maori flute thing…'

'…The Koauau,' interrupted Ruru.

'… when you went to stay with your rugby friend in Rotorua? He runs his own team there. And if you lift up your vest, I am sure I will see Hemi's name tattooed on your heart.'

Ruru's face dropped. 'A ghost?' he asked.

'I don't believe in them… at least I didn't. He told me about his fear of water. I tried to teach him to swim too.'

It was all too much for Ruru to take in. 'Did he talk about me?'

'All the time. He was...' Dai stopped for a moment, 'he is so proud of you.'

'Really?' a smile spread across Ruru's face through his fearsome tattoos and through the tears, which flooded from his eyes and weaved in between the raindrops.

'He's a good boy.'

'But why did he come to you?' asked Ruru. 'Why didn't he come back to me?'

'I don't know. I don't know why your son came back to me and why mine... well, who knows.'

'You lost your boy too?' said Ruru softly.

'Yes, I did.'

'I'm sorry, mate.'

'The mustard seed!' said Dai spontaneously.

Ruru looked confused. 'What?'

'You know about Buddhism?'

'I don't know anything,' replied Ruru. He looked at the wounds on Dai's face. 'Here, let me look at that.'

Dai allowed Ruru to inspect his cuts and bruises.

'You know what you're doing?'

'When I stopped playing rugby I became the team medic. Anyway it looks like you've broken that cheekbone...'

'I haven't broken anything,' smiled Dai. 'You're the one who clocked me.'

Ruru went to his boat, moored to the end of the boat launch and picked up a first aid kit.

They went inside the house to escape the rain and sat on the last two pieces of dining furniture left, a garden chair and footstool. As Ruru patched up Dai's wounds the atmosphere lightened. They made some small talk to try to cover over the profundity of what had just happened.

'Anyway,' said Ruru as he closed up a gash above Dai's right eye with medical strips, 'The Mustard Seed.'

'It's a Buddhist parable,' said Dai. 'One day in a village in northern India, in the time of the Buddha, a woman came screaming and crying to the Buddha. Her name was Kisa Gotami. She was carrying her dead son in her arms. It was clear to everyone in the village that the boy had been dead for some time, decay had started to set in. She pleaded with the Buddha to bring him back, she begged him to do something. So, the Buddha said, "I know a cure for death." So Kisa Gotami said, "Tell me what I have to do. I'll do anything."'

Dai winced as Ruru rubbed an antiseptic wipe over a tender open wound.

'Go on,' said Ruru.

'So the Buddha said, "Bring me a mustard seed and I will cure your son of his death. But the seed must come from a house that death has never visited." So, Kisa handed her son over to the Buddha and ran around the village to find a mustard seed. She knocked on every door and every house had a mustard seed, but none had escaped death. In the meantime the Buddha cremated the child's remains. After Kisa Gotami had gone all over the village only to meet with the same outcome each time, she came back to the Buddha and said, "How selfish my grief was."'

'So what's your point?' asked Ruru.

'I was blind too,' replied Dai. 'All I saw was my grief. I didn't see anything else. I didn't see my wife's grief, I just tried to get her to ignore it. I didn't see myself. I just tried to get on with things, pretend it didn't happen, but I couldn't see my own... empathy. I couldn't see the truth. I didn't want to see it. It was as though I was the only person to have felt pain like that. It took a little boy to come into my life to realise my own humanity again. If he can deal with death, then surely I can.'

Ruru cleaned the blood off Dai's face with a gentleness that belied all that Dai had thought of him.

'Maybe somewhere, in the heart of the Amazon there is a grieving mother or father talking to a little boy in a Welsh rugby shirt. I don't know. I don't understand it. Maybe that's where the beauty is – in not understanding everything.'

Ruru looked at Dai with a renaissance of life and love behind his eyes and smiled.

15. NEW BEGINNINGS

Some months later…

Ruru ushered the children on to the stage at Havelock Town Hall. The children, sporting faces decorated in traditional Maori patterns, shuffled with gleaming faces from the wings, looking for their families in the audience. The little ones waved enthusiastically at their mothers, fathers, brothers, sisters, aunts and uncles, while the older children did their best to show their maturity.

The weather was beautiful. A thin, indeterminate covering of wispy cloud drifted gently above the Waitangi Day celebrations. The faces of the children on the stage sported a mixture of varying expressions. Some looked nervous, desperate not to make a mistake, while others tried to contain unwanted giggles. They all looked beautiful.

Harry Stone stepped forward with his hands awkwardly at his side and in a clear, high-pitched voice addressed the audience.

'My name is Harry Stone,' he said. 'Welcome to the Havelock Waitangi Day celebrations. We hope you enjoy our presentation.'

Dai and Bronnie sat in the front row of the audience and smiled broadly. Dai reached over and held Bronnie's hand. They grasped each other tightly as they once used to. Dai could feel love flowing between them once more.

'Who would have thought?' said Bronnie.

'What?'

'That Ruru would be so good with those kids.'

Ruru joined the children on the stage in full ceremonial dress, organized the boys and called to them. The children performed the Ka Mate Haka with verve and gusto. Eyes were bulging, tongues were extended as far as possible, thighs were struck with power and the cries were heartfelt and loud. The voices echoed through Havelock Town Hall.

Following a prolonged applause, the ceremony came to close and slowly the men, women and children of Havelock began to amble out of the building. Dai felt a warmth rising within him as he watched Bronnie busily running around the hall congratulating her pupils. He had harboured thoughts that the move to New Zealand was, as many had claimed, running away. In truth, the things that he might have tried to run away from in South Wales were in New Zealand when they arrived. You take your past with you, wherever you go. But as he watched Bronnie mingling happily with new friends, he realized that Havelock was now home, and that home was where the future was.

As Dai was picking up his belongings from his front row seat, he felt a tap on his shoulder.

'I have something for you,' said Ruru.

'Good grief, Ruru.' Dai tapped his heart. 'You scared me.'

'Oh, sorry mate. Did you enjoy the show?'

'Yeah,' Dai popped his hands in his pocket. 'You've done well with the kids.'

'Yeah, it's fun.'

'It won't be long before they'll scare me more than you!'

'Oh shut up Pākehā.' Dai stopped for a while and his thoughts turned to Hemi once again. Ruru was confused. 'What?'

'It's nothing,' Dai chuckled. 'You're not the first person to call me that.'

'Anyway, as I said, I have something for you.'

'What is it?' asked Dai.

Ruru picked out a cuboid parcel wrapped in brown postage paper and handed it to Dai who quickly began tearing at the seams. He pulled out the contents, a book, and read out the title.

'A Thousand and One Arabian Nights.'

It was his own boyhood copy which he had lent to Hemi.'

'I found it in Hemi's room last week when I was clearing it out,' said Ruru.

Dai's face became more contemplative. He looked around the hall and for a moment he saw Hemi's face smiling in the crowd of children leaving the celebrations. He blinked, then he was gone. Dai smiled softly. Ruru shook Dai by the hand, pulled Dai in firmly and initiated a heartfelt hongi. As their nose and foreheads met the seeds of and unlikely friendship began to sprout.

Two weeks later...

Dai blew out the candles at the dinner table and led Bronnie by the hand to the bedroom. He stood at the foot of the bed and slowly began to undress her. He was tender and gentle. The tips of his fingers walked up and down her body with complete love and respect. He loosened the buttons on her blouse and carefully guided her arms out of the sleeves. Next, he unzipped her skirt and allowed it to fall to the floor before removing her underwear. He removed her bra, stumbling as ever on the hooks, much to the amusement of Bronnie. She allowed him the honour of touching her again and took his hand in hers and pressed it firmly against her breast. She inhaled sharply as the passion surged through her. Then with reciprocal love and respect she unbuttoned his shirt and caressed his chest. Both were shaking, trembling as if they were seeing each other naked for the very first time. Bronnie pulled her husband on the bed and guided him inside her.

'I've missed you,' she said.

'I missed you too.'

Indeed she had missed him. She had missed the strength of his hold, she had missed hearing his loving moans, feeling the warm harmonics from his deep voice resonating through her body as he held her close, and she had missed the feel of his rough hands on her silky skin.

The next day, as the sun shone through the large windows and patio doors, Dai hammered two holes in the living room wall. He placed a spirit level on the pencil line, which ran horizontally between the two and saw the bubble line up perfectly. Then he picked up a picture of Bronnie, Ieuan and himself and placed it with pride on the wall. He stood back and admired not only his handy-work, but also the happiness in the picture.

At that point, the patio doors opened and in walked Bronnie holding Harry Stone's hand. The child looked nervous. He held in one hand a rucksack and some school books in the other.

'Harry, this is my husband, Dai,' said Bronnie.

Harry placed his bag on the floor, stepped forward and offered his hand.

'Hello Mr Ifans.'

'So…' Dai took in a deep breath. 'You'll be staying with us then.'

Harry seemed a little nervous. 'Umm…'

Dai took the rucksack from the boy. 'Ok this is a good time to talk about ground rules.'

'Oh, Dai! No!' said Bronnie rolling her eyes. 'We can do that another…'

Dai interrupted. 'No, now! Right, young man, in this house you will call me Dai! It's my name. If I should stub my toe on the sofa, spill my coffee at the table or fart uncontrollably, you may then refer to me as a berk or bum-head…'

'Dai!' erupted Bronnie behind restrained laughter, while Harry's laughter was much louder.

'You will refer to Bronnie as the old woman who lived in a shoe...'

'Dai!' shouted Bronnie, much to the amusement of Harry.

'And finally... always, always eat your bogies!'

Harry roared while Bronnie scowled menacingly at him. 'Dai,' she said, 'too far!'

As Dai showed Harry to his new room, Bronnie looked up at the picture hanging on the wall, sighed and began to do what she had been unable to do since losing Ieuan; live.

ABOUT THE AUTHOR

Jon Lawrence was born in Pontypridd, South Wales and studied at Leeds University and Sheffield University where he read music and ethnomusicology. Having lectured in music for fifteen years he now writes novels, plays, essays and poetry. His first novel, The Pastoral and novella Albatross Bay have received rave reviews from Amazon readers. He teaches music, poetry and creative writing to children of all ages. Having visited New Zealand in 2010 and 2011 he developed a profound interest in Maori culture and fell in love with the country. This interest informed this book. Jon Lawrence lives in Norfolk, England.

*For more information on Jon Lawrence visit
www.lawrencewriting.net*

Also Available

The Pastoral

Albatross Bay

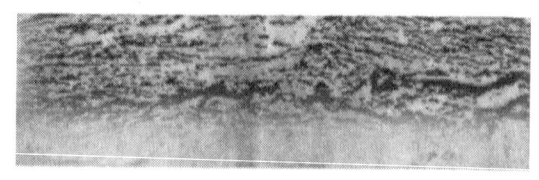

Made in the USA
Charleston, SC
25 May 2016